THE GHOSTLY GROUNDS:

DISASTER

AND

DESSERT

(A CANINE CASPER COZY MYSTERY—BOOK 6)

SOPHIE LOVE

Sophie Love

#1 bestselling author Sophie Love is author of THE INN AT SUNSET HARBOR romantic comedy series, which includes eight books; of THE ROMANCE CHRONICLES romantic comedy series, which includes five books; of the new CANINE CASPER cozy mystery series, which included six books; and of the new CURIOUS BOOKSTORE cozy mystery series, which included five books (and counting).

Sophie would love to hear from you, so please visit www.sophieloveauthor.com to email her, to join the mailing list, to receive free ebooks, to hear the latest news, and to stay in touch!

ISBN: 978-1-0943-9163-2

BOOKS BY SOPHIE LOVE

A CURIOUS BOOKSTORE COZY MYSTERY
THE WITCHING PLACE: A FATAL FOLIO (Book #1)
THE WITCHING PLACE: MURDER BY MANUSCRIPT (Book #2)
THE WITCHING PLACE: A PERILOUS PAGE (Book #3)
THE WITCHING PLACE: A VANISHED VOLUME (Book #4)
THE WITCHING PLACE: A TAINTED TOME (Book #5)

THE CANINE CASPER COZY MYSTERY SERIES
THE GHOSTLY GROUNDS: MURDER AND BREAKFAST (Book #1)
THE GHOSTLY GROUNDS: DEATH AND BRUNCH (Book #2)
THE GHOSTLY GROUNDS: MALICE AND LUNCH (Book #3)
THE GHOSTLY GROUNDS: VENGEANCE AND DINNER (Book #4)
THE GHOSTLY GROUNDS: SCANDAL AND SUPPER (Book #5)
THE GHOSTLY GROUNDS: DISASTER AND DESSERT (Book #6)

THE INN AT SUNSET HARBOR
FOR NOW AND FOREVER (Book #1)
FOREVER AND FOR ALWAYS (Book #2)
FOREVER, WITH YOU (Book #3)
IF ONLY FOREVER (Book #4)
FOREVER AND A DAY (Book #5)
FOREVER, PLUS ONE (Book #6)
FOR YOU, FOREVER (Book #7)
CHRISTMAS FOREVER (Book #8)

THE ROMANCE CHRONICLES
LOVE LIKE THIS (Book #1)
LOVE LIKE THAT (Book #2)
LOVE LIKE OURS (Book #3)
LOVE LIKE THEIRS (Book #4)
LOVE LIKE YOURS (Book #5)

CHAPTER ONE

Come home.

That's what Marie had written back to her mother in response to the postcard that had arrived at June Manor several weeks ago. Marie had sent it not even knowing if her nomadic mother would get it. And even if she did, Abagail Fortune would have no way of knowing it was from her daughter and not her aunt, June.

Come home. It seemed so poetic and dumb all at the same time. But now that Marie was standing at the front door, looking out to a mother she had not seen in over thirty years, those two words seemed to hold an impossible amount of weight.

"Mom?" Marie said.

Abagail Fortune tilted her head slightly and tears filled her eyes immediately. "Marie? My God, Marie, is that you?"

Marie did not trust herself to speak, so she only nodded as her mother stepped into June Manor and wrapped her arms around her. Marie's first reaction was to pull away, to distance herself from the woman that had abandoned her and her father—the woman that had never bothered to locate her or to find her. It was almost like hugging a stranger for a moment. After all, the only reason she was standing here right now was because she had sent a postcard to June and apparently thought June was the one that had written back the simple two-word response.

Oh God, Marie thought. *She doesn't even know June is dead...*

But then Marie slowly gave in to the craving she'd been feeling for some faraway ghost since the age of twelve, when her mother had stepped out of her life. She returned the hug and thought it felt strange; there was a sense of closure—of a book being closed and another one being immediately opened. Despite this sensation, there was still a degree of hurt, though. She'd waited so long...wondering if this moment would ever arrive and now that it was here she was still angry. She hadn't quite expected that.

"Marie," her mother gasped as she broke the hug and looked her daughter in the eyes for the first time in nearly three decades. "What are you doing here? Visiting Aunt June?"

"Sort of," Marie said, still not quite trusting herself to speak. "What are *you* doing here?"

"Well, I sent a postcard to June and she responded back with a very plain and simple message—which is not like June. She just said to come home. I figured something was wrong and then…and then here *you* are." She stopped here, pausing for a moment and then looked inside the house for the first time, looking behind Marie. "Is everything okay here?"

Not exactly the ideal way to speak with your mother for the first time in thirty years, Marie thought. But she knew what she had to do. As if sensing some great sadness in the air, Boo came trotting to the door from elsewhere inside the house; her dog had become the closest thing she'd had to family over the past six or seven months, and he seemed to know it.

"Come in, Mom," Marie said. She surprised herself when she reached out and took her mother's hand. "There are some things I need to tell you."

***

The half hour that followed was sad, joyous, and a little surreal for Marie. She found herself sitting in the very room she'd once daydreamed in while her mother and Aunt June gossiped and laughed. Only now, she was sitting in Aunt June's chair and her mother was right across from her. And while her Great Aunt June was absent from the picture, her presence was very much felt. It did not take long for the very loaded question to come up. Hearing it from her mother's mouth was about the same as hearing a shotgun blast in the same room.

"So where's June?" Abagail asked.

"Mom…I don't know how to tell you this. She…well, Aunt June passed away."

The joy on her mother's face slowly crumpled. The tears were coming before the joy was completely gone. Abagail placed a hand to her mouth and let out a little gasp. Marie found herself sitting rigidly in her seat, not sure how her mother would react to the news.

"How?" Abagail finally managed to get out.

Marie spoke slowly, wanting to give her mother time to understand it and process it all at the same time. She told her mother about getting the call from Sherriff Miles (still a deputy back then) and the news she had received from Aunt June's lawyer when she arrived in town for the funeral. By then, the tears were still spilling but Abagail seemed to have control of herself.

"She left the house to me," Marie said. "And the moment I moved in…well, my life was pretty shaken up."

"So…this house is yours now?"

"Yeah. I've been running it as a bed and breakfast for the past several months."

The look of excitement and pride on her mother's face was something she had never expected to see. In the awed silence that followed, Posey came quietly into the room, asking no questions and making no comments; she simply served the women tea and made her way back towards the dining room, Marie could sense her lurking just at the edges, perhaps making sure any guests that happened to come down did not disturb the conversation. Marie supposed Posey had also become something very much like family. Rebeka, too.

Maybe, she thought as Boo lay at her feet and Posey quietly spoke with a guest in the kitchen, *I have more family than I thought.*

"How's business?" Abagail asked, wiping the tears away. Marie was sure there would be more questions about June later, but for now it seemed her mother was trying to choose joy. Or maybe she was trying to avoid the fact that June had died and she had been nowhere nearby to know about it.

"It's been very good," she said. "That hasn't always been the case, but…well, it's a pretty long story."

Abagail nodded, looking around the room and sipping from her tea before turning her eyes back to Marie. "I won't lie," she said, fighting off more tears. "It makes for a pretty terrible Christmas surprise to heat about June, but you…seeing *you* is just about the best gift I could ever get."

"Don't do that, Mom," Marie said. The words were out of her mouth before she could stop them. She looked to her mother, standing just to the right of the Christmas tree she and Robbie had put up about a week ago. Her mind wanted to go to Robbie and latch on to how she had basically dismissed him the previous night, but her entire brain was bogged down with thoughts of her mother. Her life felt as if it had been turned upside down and now she needed to find out if she wanted to flip it right-side up again.

"Don't do what?" Abagail asked.

"Pretend you missed me…that you're happy to see me."

"But I am!" She nearly yelled this response and Marie was surprised and a little guilt-stricken to see genuine hurt in her mother's face.

"You left, Mom," Marie said. She was on her feet now, too, though she could not quite remember standing. "You left me and Dad, and when Dad died, I barely saw you out of the corner of my eye at his funeral. And I've heard *nothing* from you. I didn't know if you were alive or dead…not until I came here."

"Here?" Abagail asked.

"I found some of your postcards. Aunt June kept them and—," she stopped here, her heart still trying to decide on anger, reconciliation, or sadness. Currently, it was grasping for all and Marie simply couldn't handle it. "You know what? No. I can't do this with you right now. I'm not answering *your* questions. I have far too many for you."

"Okay, so ask them."

"Why did you do it?" Marie asked before her mother had even finished her sentence.

"The easy answer is because I was selfish. But there is a larger answer at play, too. One that I don't know you'll understand."

"A larger answer that had you travelling all over the world?" Marie contested. "Seems to me you just wanted away from the responsibilities of a family and wanted to go off and live this adventurous life. I guess a husband and daughter just held you back from all of that, huh?"

Abagail nodded, looking away from Marie. "I suppose I deserve that. But no…my main purpose was not to just live up some marvelous life that I didn't think you and your father would allow. I had to…"

She stopped here and Marie could tell that she was struggling with something. It was more than just looking for the right words; it appeared that she was trying to make the decision to say what was on her mind. In the end, she decided to say it. When she did, she still could not look directly at Marie. Instead, she looked at the Christmas tree, as if she'd found a particular ornament that had caught her attention.

"I had to find out some things about myself," she finally finished.

"Don't make me puke," Marie said. "You needed to travel the world for *thirty years* to find yourself?"

"No, not like that. Not in the cheesy poetic way. No. There's something I needed to come to terms with and…God, I don't know."

Marie thought of those post cards, of her simple little response of *Come home* and, God forgive her, she wished she'd never sent the damned thing. At least a little bit; there was still that young girl inside of her that had missed her mother desperately.

"You know what, Mom," Marie said. "It's been thirty years without you. I think I can spend the next thirty the same way. So maybe you should—"

"Wait," Abagail said. "Hold on. How long have you lived here?"

Marie rolled her eyes at her mother's flippant question. "Almost seven months now."

Abagail eyed her daughter in a cautious sort of way and then looked around the room—not only around the room, but also out into the hallway, into the dining room and the attached hall.

"So then, you know by now, I'd think, right?"

"Know what?" Marie asked, irritated.

For the first time since Marie had started speaking about Aunt June's passing, Abagail Fortune smiled. It was a thin smile and made her look rather striking. It also made her look like the sort of woman that was very good at keeping secrets.

"You mean to tell me you've been here for seven months and you haven't seen a ghost yet?"

Marie wasn't sure what to say or what to think. Her first thought was that her mother was lying to her. Surely she'd heard some of June's stories about the house and was trying to play on her emotions. But at the same time, she thought of the diaries she'd found in the hidden upstairs room. Her mother had been mentioned a few times and there were a hell of a lot of ghosts in those diaries.

"Marie?"

Marie blinked, startled. She wondered how long she'd been lost in her own thoughts. She found her mother still looking at her, uncertain.

"Marie…do you have it, too?"

"Have what?" she asked. Her voice was soft and quiet, and she knew the answer before her mother spoke it.

"I don't know," Abagail said. "I suppose some might call it a gift. I think *gift* is an odd word for it, but I don't know what else to call it. But what I mean is…you can sense them, can't you? The dead?"

Marie was shocked when she found herself nodding. As she nodded, her mother's eyes started to brim with tears. "Can you...can you *see* them? Can you interact with them?"

Now Marie felt her own tears coming on and she had no idea why. All she knew for sure was that her mother was stepping towards her and tears were coming down her cheeks. She did not look sad, but almost happy. And for reasons Marie could not understand, she wanted her mother to hold her again. Just two minutes ago, she'd wanted her mother out of the house. And now...now what? The mention of ghosts had done something—the mention of a *gift.*

"I would have never imagined it..." Abagail said. "To think I've spent all of this time looking for answers and they've been right here, with you, all along."

CHAPTER TWO

The weight of the conversation felt too heavy for the small room. More than that, Marie felt like it was almost suffocating to have it there, in the house. It was odd, but it almost felt like gossiping about someone that was in the same room. Both wiping tears away, Marie and Abagail Fortune each grabbed a thermos of coffee, bundled up, and headed outside.

That's how Marie ended up spending the morning of Christmas Eve on the very chilly beach along Port Bliss, Maine. The cold had bite, but it was not overly bitter. The frigid waves crashed along the shore and though she could feel her cheeks reddening from the cold almost right away, she could have stood there forever. The ocean against the cold somehow felt surreal—like the entire morning had so far. Her mother beside her, hot coffee in her hands, and secrets starting to spill out of a chest that had been closed for nearly thirty years.

"It was your Great Aunt June that opened my eyes to the fact that I had it," Abagail said. "I was fourteen or so and, as you might imagine, your grandmother did not take kindly to June telling me spooky stories. But I remember there was this one night during my sophomore year of college at NYU, walking back home from a party. I was going through the lobby of a dorm and saw two men standing by a window. They were transparent, and one of them had blood on his face. I knew they were ghosts. I'd seen ghosts before, but these were different, I felt a pull to them, like they wanted help. It freaked me out and I hopped on a bus the next morning. I stayed with June for a few days and she helped me sort it all out."

"So you've had it since you were a kid?" Marie asked.

"I think so. I mean, all kids have imaginary friends, but I would *really* see people that others weren't seeing. It was usually in smaller, quiet places but every now and then it would be somewhere like on the street or even one time, when I was eight or nine, in a movie theater."

Marie tried to take all of this in, tried to believe it all. A lot of it sounded like what she had read in June's diaries. And while it was amazing and eerie to know that her mother had the same gift, it still did not answer the deeper questions. Marie wasn't so sure her mother wasn't just using this (if it was true at all) to dodge those questions.

"Okay, so let's say I believe you," Marie said. "How does that line up with you abandoning your family?"

Abagail looked out to the ocean and sipped her coffee. The cold breeze was whipping her hair in a way that reminded Marie quite a bit of June.

"Your father knew about what I could do, but I don't know that he ever believed me," she explained. "He was never rude or mean to me. Your father was one of the kindest men I ever met and it hurt me to leave him. But I had to. It got to a point where I would hear and see ghosts everywhere I went. Sometimes even when we were at home, I could hear them calling. Your father thought there might be something wrong with me—some mental issues. But I took a variety of tests that all came back clean. It just started to wear on our marriage and…I know it sounds bad and I *do* regret it, but I made the decision to leave. He just kept pressuring me to get more tests. Even June insisted on it for a time. But after a while, I think the trust between your father and I just dissolved. I told myself back then that leaving would be easier on you and your father—and on me, for sure."

"But you never reached out later," Marie argued. "You could have at least come to speak to me after Dad's funeral."

"And I should have. But by the time I finally came to terms with what was happening to me, I convinced myself it was too late. I stayed away because I didn't want to come back six years later to disrupt whatever sense of peace and normalcy you and your father had managed to find." She paused here for a second and then added, quietly: "Do you know the Dairy Queen we all used to go to when you were little? The one where you'd get the mint chocolate chip blizzards?"

The memory of it stung deep, but Marie nodded.

"I sat in my car in that parking lot for about two hours, trying to build up the courage to visit you. But I had no answers for you. The only answers I had were the ones I've just given you. I felt embarrassed and ashamed and, honestly, I didn't have my own answers, either. Not all of them, anyway. So I left, not wanting to be a burden on you. I left…and I've hated myself for it ever since."

"Where did you go?" Marie asked, not wanting to fixate on the part about her hating herself. She then shook her head, stopped walking, and sighed. "Scratch that. Because of the postcards, I know where you went. You went all over—different parts of the world. *That's* why I said it seemed like you just wanted to travel and not have a family."

"Oh, I did travel. I travelled a lot. But I was looking for answers the entire time. I was finding people that had this same gift and trying to figure out how to either get rid of it or how to refine it so that it wasn't so all-consuming."

"And did you find the answers you were looking for?" Marie asked with only a little bitterness in her tone.

"I think I did," Abagail said. "And now that I know you have it…maybe I can help you."

It was beyond appealing to Marie but she was also very hesitant to let her mother know she needed her for anything. Instead, she looked out to the ocean and admitted something out loud that she had only spoke internally to herself since she was a child.

"I felt abandoned," Marie said. "I felt like you had left me because Dad and I weren't' enough."

"Marie, no…"

Abagail stepped forward, her arms extended, but Marie shook her head. There was still a skirmish taking place inside of her, half of her still wanting to push her mother away, another half wanting to instantly start working at repairing things. It was just too hard to get a handle on.

"No. Not yet. I just…I want to show you something."

"Okay…"

And without saying anything else, Marie turned away from the sea and started back towards June Manor. She could hear her mother walking across the sand and then, after the little wooden walkways between the beach and the back yard, she could hear her on the grass. She was leading her mother to the outside seating area that Benjamin had finished only days ago. There were two benches, built-in flower beds, decorative rock walls, and a rustic-looking fire pit within the little area. There were other built-in areas for more elaborate flower displays once the weather got warmer.

"How old is the addition?" Abagail asked.

"It was just finished a few days ago," Marie said. "But I'm showing you this because I'm curious…looking at the house and then at where we're standing, does this area mean anything to you?"

"No," Abagail said. "I mean, it looks gorgeous. You've done a remarkable job and I think June would approve, but…no. Why? Should it?"

"I don't know. Come with me one more time."

This time, Marie led her mother back inside. They went up the patio stairs and back through the kitchen. Both Posey and Rebeka were in the dining room. Rebeka looked almost embarrassed, as if she knew she was in the midst of some huge moment in which she did not belong. Posey, on the other hand, looked to Abagail Fortune with skepticism and gave off protective vibes.

Fortunately, they did not walk into the dining room to give Posey the opportunity to become protective. Marie led her mother into the basement and walked directly to the doorway to the hidden room that had recently been uncovered.

"Did you know this was here, by any chance?" Marie asked.

"This door? No…it looks new. Did you not put it there?"

"Oh, I had it installed when my contractor exposed a hidden underground room when he was doing the additions."

"Hidden…?"

Marie opened the door and stepped aside to let her mother in. Marie flipped on the light switch the electrician had installed. It was the only electricity in the room. She had seen it enough in the past few days, so it actually looked rather drab to her: the walls of brick and cinderblock, the floor that had been pretty awful when discovered but then mostly repaired with wood by Benjamin. It was a plain room, except for the peculiar shelves on the wall and the chest sitting against the left wall.

"What was in here when you found it?" Abagail asked.

"Nothing but that chest."

"Anything in it?"

"I have no idea. I don't have a key and I just can't bring myself to bust it open."

Abagail stepped into the room and looked around, amazed. "This house…I always thought it was full of mystery. I mean, June was enough of a mystery, but this house always had a certain feel to it." She grinned and then glanced back to Marie. "Any more secrets?"

She nearly said yes, thinking of the room that had been hidden, the upstairs bedroom at the end of the hall. But that was where she had kept her strange little timeline, the rough historical map she'd tried to piece together based on her mother's postcards to Aunt June. For now, she thought she'd keep that to herself.

"A few," she finally answered. "But for now, I think I'd like to keep them for myself."

Abagail looked disappointed but did not argue. She walked to the trunk against the wall and ran her hand over its top. She eyed the lock with the sort of anticipation a child might give to a present under the Christmas tree.

"Hey, Mom?" Marie asked. She knew what she was about to ask and had no idea where it was coming from. It certainly wasn't a product of her heart because her heart was still all over the place. If there was indeed some form of spirit within the human body, she supposed it might be coming from there.

"Yes?" Abagail asked.

"You responded to what you thought was Aunt June asking you to come home. What were your plans after that?"

"I was hoping to spend Christmas with her," she answered sadly. "Maybe stay through New Year's. But now…"

"Now you're going to enjoy a complimentary week-long stay at June Manor," Marie interrupted. "We don't exactly have a concierge or bag boy, so go grab your bags."

CHAPTER THREE

Marie wasn't quite sure where Rebeka had been hiding her guitar—or her slightly-above-average ability to play it—but she was pleasantly surprised later that afternoon when she brought it downstairs and starting playing Christmas songs on it. She started with "Oh, Holy Night," and transitioned into "We Wish You a Merry Christmas." She had an almost folksy tone to her voice, but something a bit sweeter. It was like a remix of Janis Joplin and Taylor Swift in an odd, holiday miracle sort of way.

"Where did you learn to play like that?" Marie asked as one lingering guest, Abagail, and Posey applauded.

"YouTube tutorials," Rebeka answered. "I've been watching them for the last few months."

It was an answer that made Marie realize just how preoccupied she'd been as of late; she'd never even known Rebeka even had a guitar, much less that she could play it well.

"You think you could save a few songs for tomorrow morning?" Marie asked. "If you guys don't have anything else to do, I'd love to have you spend Christmas at June Manor." It was something she'd been considering for most of the day—not only because Rebeka and Posey truly did feel like family, but because the thought of spending quality time alone with a mother that had been absent for thirty years during Christmas morning was a bit too much to comprehend.

"That's so sweet," Rebeka said. "I'd love to! Thanks, Marie!"

"Not me," Posey said. "I've got to wake up far too early in the morning to make it up to Augusta for my family's usual get-together. However, if it goes the way most of my family Christmases go, I'll be here around six tomorrow afternoon to drink copious amounts of wine and to do a lot of griping. Have the cab company on speed dial, would you?"

In a surprising twist, though, Marie thought her mother's sudden presence almost made it feel more like a family Christmas. The woman still did not *feel* like family, but June Manor seemed to be mending something between them. As they sat the sitting room, listening to

Christmas music on Spotify and chatting, Marie found it easy to imagine Aunt June's ghost peeking around corners and enjoying the sight of this reunion. That idea alone made Marie very happy—and happier still when she realized it was happening in front of a Christmas tree.

"So, Rebeka," Abagail asked as she sipped from a glass of red wine. "I gather that you're living here, is that correct?"

"Yes, ma'am," Rebeka said. "I was in a very bad place when Marie hired me and she just…well, she's got an enormous heart. She's allowed me to stay here for a few months now while I get back on my feet."

Abagail looked to Marie with a sense of pride, smiling warmly. "I won't even pretend she gets that from me. That's her father, one hundred percent."

It was odd and a little hurtful to hear her mother mention her father but Marie barely had time to register the comment before Rebeka was speaking again.

"And I suppose now, on Christmas Eve, is the best time for me to give her an update," Rebeka said, looking almost comically at Marie. "Because of your generosity and my willingness to pawn off just about half of my belongings, I'm finally able to afford a place of my own. I love it here, and I love you, but I'll be looking for apartments at the beginning of the year."

Marie wasn't quite sure how to feel about this. All she knew was that she was walking across the room to hug her right away. She was proud of Rebeka in that she was finally able to take this huge step, but she also knew that she was going to miss her terribly.

"One question, though," Rebeka said. "Can I still have the job?"

"Of course you can," Marie said, hugging her tightly and doing her best to fight off tears. "I'd be very sad if you left June Manor altogether."

It was a sweet moment, made slightly awkward by the presence of her mother. Her mother did not know Rebeka, she did not know the things they'd been through together as June Manor had grown. Yet somehow, she was very glad that her mother could see some of the friendships she had made and what her life was like now. It created a rather peaceful feeling that seemed to radiate through most of the house, making the Christmas cheer a bit more special.

Apparently, Rebeka could sense that there was unfinished business between Marie and Abagail, though. Yes, there was cheer and peace in the house, but the tension and awkwardness between mother and daughter was quite clear, too. So, with her bombshell dropped and endearing hug from Marie received, Rebeka gave a thin smile and nodded towards the stairs.

"I'm going to head on up," she said. "I'm pretty much just a big kid at Christmas and I'm sure I'll be up super early. Ms. Fortune, it was so nice to meet you."

"You, too, dear. Merry Christmas."

Rebeka gave Marie one last hug and then bound up the stairs with her guitar in hand.

"She seems like a sweetheart," Abagail said once Rebeka's footsteps had receded into nothing upstairs.

"She really is," Marie said. "She and Posey both. There's no way I could have made it this far without their help."

"You've really made something of this place, that's for sure," Abagail said. "I mean, I've always loved coming here, but you've given it an...well I don't know *exactly* what it is. It just feels warm and inviting. Again, I have to say, I think June would love it."

"Oh, apparently she does," Marie said rather conspiratorial. "She likes it enough to poke her head in every now and then."

"June?" Abagail said, sitting up straight, he eyes going wide. "She's still around?"

"Sometimes. Just like when she was alive, she just seems to come and go when she pleases. Come to think of it, though, I haven't seen her in about a week or so." Saying this out loud brought a question go her mind. It was a big question, and one she felt she probably shouldn't even ask. But once she'd formed it, she had to. If not, she knew it would never leave her alone. "Did you ever see Dad?" she asked. "After he died, I mean?"

Abagail shook her head. "No. You?"

"No. All of this ghost stuff is new to me. It's like Port Bliss or June Manor sort of activated it in me. But you...you've had it forever. How did you live with it?"

Abagail shrugged. "It's one of the reasons I travelled so much. Part of it was trying to escape it, I guess. But most of it was because I was looking for others that had the gift. I wanted to figure out how to live with it as if it were a blessing and not a curse."

"And did you figure it out?"

"I think so. It cost me nearly twenty-five years, a marriage, and a daughter, but I did."

Marie wasn't quite sure why, but this comment softened her heart a bit. It helped her to see that her mother had come to terms with what she had done, but it did not mean that she was okay with how things had turned out by any means. She's made sacrifices to get her answers and stayed away from her family to make things easier on them. She was sure it had to be hard…had to have been gut-wrenching at times.

"Mom, if I'm being honest," she said, speaking before she was aware the words were even coming out, "it will always hurt. But you're here now and we haven't screamed each other's heads off yet. I think we can stop with the self-abuse. Stop beating yourself up."

"If you'll allow it, I think I *have to* for a while," Abagail said, wiping a tear away from her eye. "I came here expecting June. The absolute last person I expected to see was you and it…well, it's rocked me. And I think it's the universe's way of telling me that I can get another chance with you…if you believe in that sort of thing."

Marie smiled, looking around the sitting room. "Oh, you'd be impressed with some of the things I've started to believe since moving here."

Abagail smiled and nodded to the Christmas tree. There were only a few present under it—gifts to and from Posey, Rebeka, and Marie, along with small gifts from a few local businesses. But it twinkled and gleamed as if it held treasures for an entire family beneath it.

"Things like Santa, perhaps?" Abagail said.

Marie laughed out loud and said, "You know…I think in this house, anything is possible."

***

Marie really wished she'd known Rebeka played guitar before buying her Christmas gift. When Rebeka opened her gift card to a local spa, she seemed genuinely overjoyed, but Marie hated to give impersonal gifts. The spa gift card was not nearly as personal and thought-out as the gift Rebeka had given her: two books wrapped together with a ribbon; the first was *These Old Haunts: A Recorded History of Seaside Hauntings Along America's East Coast* and the second was *101 Tricks for Your Unique Dog.* The ghost book looked like it had come from a specialized bookshop and bore a printing date of 1965.

"Rebeka, this is perfect," she said. And as she gave her a huge hug (apparently a trend over this holiday season), she noticed that her mother had picked up *These Old Haunts* and was looking at it with much interest.

As promised, Rebeka pulled out her guitar a bit later and played a few songs, even if it *was* just the three of them. Boo was quite curious about the guitar and made a habit of sniffing at the strings between songs. After that, they had a lazy lunch of leftovers and cleaned up all the wrapping paper from that morning. Afterwards, there wasn't much talking; Marie watched as her mother made her way slowly through the house, taking a tour of her past. Abagail seemed to go from moments of happiness and whimsy to a forlorn sort of regret. Those slow hours contributed to Christmas Day winding itself down in that bittersweet way it always does.

"I just can't believe she's really gone," Abagail would say from time to time as she made her way through the rooms.

Marie joined her later in the day as she ventured into the additions Benjamin had just finished before Christmas. Marie herself hadn't quite gotten used to them. It was odd to not have the downstairs hallway end where it was once had. But Benjamin and the interior decorators had done an amazing job of making the new entryway, small lobby area, and three rooms look just like the remainder of the house.

"I don't know you well enough to know if you enjoy the occasional cheesy sentiment," Abagail said. "I know as a girl, you used to laugh at just about everything...but how are you with cheesy sentiment?"

"I tend to roll my eyes," Marie said. "But let's see what you've got."

Abagail was standing in the perfectly square lobby of the new addition. A bench sat along the center wall, and the other wall was adorned with two chairs and a small book case. It was perfectly cozy...another way it was just like the rest of the house.

"This might be the best Christmas present I could have gotten," Abagail said. "Well, aside from an unexpected reunion with you. To see this house transformed and June's memory sort of living on and thriving..."

Marie surprised herself when she went to her mother, hugged her tightly, and said, "Just call me Santa."

They stood like that for a while and when Boo ventured in to see what all the commotion was about, even he turned around and left them alone to their private moment.

***

Posey was just about as joyous on Christmas Day as Marie thought she'd be. When she came by at 6:30 in the afternoon, she was just as promised. She looked aggravated and was carrying two bottles of red wine. After presents were exchanged, she sat down with Marie in the sitting room, sipping on tea and listening to quiet Christmas tunes.

"Where's your mother?" Posey asked, looking around the room suspiciously. She then realized that the answer may not be so simple and cringed. "Oh, I'm so sorry. It was not my place to ask…"

"It's okay," Marie said, perfectly understanding the afterthought. "She didn't leave again. Well, not for good. She took Boo out in my car. She said she wanted to look around the town and get reacquainted. But I thought you'd want to vent about your family. I was expecting some juicy insults."

"Meh…it's Christmas. I'll take it easy on those overbearing, jealous, loud and obnoxious imbeciles." She sipped from her third glass of wine and asked: "Boo went with her willingly?"

"He did. He seems to really like her."

"And how about you? I know this was sudden and, please forgive me for saying so, I've never heard you say a single positive thing about your mother. How are you holding up?"

"Better than I should be," Marie said. She was surprised to realize that she meant it. The resentment and hesitation were still there, but it had all shrunk down enough to also allow in some excitement. Her mother had turned back up after all these years and it turned out that deep down, she may not be quite as selfish as Marie had always expected.

"Do you think there could be reconciliation there?" Posey asked.

Marie didn't answer this question as quickly. She knew what she *wanted* to say but she also knew that a day and a half was not quite enough to properly gaze a mother-daughter relationship that had a thirty year chunk missing. Still, she hesitantly answered: "I really think there might be."

And, like most things in her life as of late, it was both terrifying and exhilarating at the same time. But she also knew that ever since moving to June Manor, surprises tended to come in pairs—or even threes. And she was almost afraid to even consider what that next surprise might be.

CHAPTER FOUR

On December 27th, Abagail came into the sitting room where Marie was reading a book and sipping on coffee. The cheer of Christmas still clung to the air and Marie was happy to find that it seemed to be helping relieve some of the awkwardness of the blossoming relationship with her mother. At first, she assumed the mischievous smile on her face was the product of some of that leftover Christmas cheer. But she soon found out that was not really the case at all.

"It's been a while since I've been in Port Bliss," Abagail said. "But I'm assuming Red Reef Diner is still open, correct?"

The mere mention of the diner brought Robbie to mind—and with images of Robbie, a bit of guilt and heartbreak, though *she* had been the one to end things. Before those thoughts could run rampant, she answered: "Yes, it's still open."

"They still have that to-die-for hot chocolate?"

"Oh yeah."

"Then let's go. I've nearly forgotten just how good that hot chocolate is."

Marie had not been to Red Reef since she had halted any momentum towards a relationship she and Robbie might have. She almost argued against going, but that would be silly. They weren't middle schoolers that had just had a spat. They were grown adults that were able to go on with their lives. And beyond that, Marie simply didn't feel like getting into the details of it all with her mother.

"Yeah, I think that's a great idea," Marie said, bookmarking her book and getting up to grab her coat.

They headed out, Boo whining to go along. Marie decided to leave him, though; with the shaky state of things between her and Robbie, she did not want to seek any favors in allowing Boo into the restaurant, even if it was through the back, as Robbie had done a few times in the past.

It was too cold to even consider walking, so they drove. On the way, Marie held her silence on her recent past with Robbie Dunne. She began to realize that it wasn't just to avoid the conversation with her mother, but also because she hadn't been quite certain about her own conflicting feelings towards another man—Brendan Peck. Thinking of Brendan as they made their way to the diner, she supposed her mother would have a multitude of questions to ask him and topics to discuss. With her mother's past and Brendan's career and interests, they'd be two peas in a pod.

When Marie and her mother stepped in through the front door of Red Reef Diner, Abagail released an audible sigh. Marie noticed that her eyes started to glisten with tears. Marie was feeling some sort of way, too. This would be the first time she'd seen Robbie (if he was on shift) since she'd ended things with him four days ago. She did her best to hide the slight anxiety she felt as they selected one of the open booths near the back.

One of the waitresses came over swiftly. Because of her involvement with Robbie, Marie recognized all of the faces. As the waitress took their order—a pretty young thing surely not much more than twenty years of age—Marie tried to tell if the woman was being snide to her. She wondered if Robbie had bothered telling everyone that the almost-relationship he'd had with her had come to an end. If this was the case, the waitress wasn't showing any signs. She took their orders cheerfully and took them directly behind the counter.

"This place hasn't changed a bit," Abagail said. "Well, I mean, it has…the tables are clearly new and it just looks cleaner. But it *feels* the same."

"I felt the same way when I came in for the first time," Marie said. "And, as I said, the hot chocolate follows suit."

"So you *do* remember coming here as a girl?" Abagail asked

"Of course I do."

"And do you remember playing with little Robbie Dunne? He was always pestering you to play toy cars with him, or to color and do those word scrambles that used to be on the back of the kids' menus."

"Yeah, I remember," Marie said quickly.

Abagail smiled widely and shook her head. "Your face just went about five shades of red," she said. "Anything I need to be filled in on?"

"Not exactly…"

"Well, then, if not Robbie Dunne, what *is* your dating situation like?"

“A little too complicated to dive into after thirty years apart,” she said with a smile. One thing she was very pleased about was finding that her mother had the same sarcastic sense of humor she had. Abagail knew right away there was no harm meant in the seemingly back-handed comment.

“What about *you?”* Marie asked. And then, realizing what she had just asked, shook her head. “Never mind. I retract that question, Maybe later but…right now, it’s just too soon.”

“Believe it or not, I’ve always loved your father,” Abagail said. “I never remarried. There were a few men I dated here and there, but nothing serious.”

Marie nodded but did not say anything, hoping it clued her mother into the fact that she *really* didn’t want to get into this conversation. Fortunately, the awkward moment was broken by the delivery of their hot chocolate and slabs of cherry pie. Much to Marie’s chagrin, though, they were brought over by none other than Robbie.

“Hey, Marie,” Robbie said, giving her a smile that seemed more rehearsed than genuine. She was also a little heartbroken to see hints of genuine sadness in his eyes.

“Hey,” she said, doing her best to meet his eyes, Then, unable to resist the opportunity, she nodded to her mother and added: “Robbie, do you by any chance know who this young lady is?”

Robbie looked at Abagail, then back to Marie. He took a step back, a smile forming on his face. “Well, she doesn’t look quite the same without June sitting beside her, but I do believe this is your mother.”

“That’s right,” Abagail said. “Robbie, it’s nice to see you again after so long. You’ve grown up into quite a handsome man.”

“Thank you, ma’am.”

“How are your folks?”

“Living elsewhere these days,” Robbie said. “I sort of inherited the diner and they started enjoying retirement. It’s been about seven or eight years now.”

“Well please let them know I said hello the next time you speak with them.”

“I absolutely will,” he said as he stepped away. He gave Marie a *holy crap* sort of look before turning his back and heading for the kitchen area.

“Yeah, okay,” Abagail said. “There’s *something* going on there…”

“There *was,”* Marie said. “But there isn’t anymore.”

"And why not?" It was clear that she was asking only to give Marie a hard time, not out of being pushy or overly nosy. That was the reason Marie entertained the conversation at all.

"It just didn't work out. When we tried things out, there was a lot of stuff going on with me and the house and—"

"By *stuff*, do you mean 'another man' by any chance?" Abagail asked with a smile.

"Wow. You're really digging aren't you?"

Abagail smiled and something about it filled Marie's heart with a warmth she had not felt in quite some time. Marie prepared to start telling her about Brendan—about the entire odd love triangle she'd been navigating through while trying to come to terms with her supernatural abilities. But before she could put that train of thought into order, there was another interruption. And this one was not nearly as pleasant as the previous one.

"You're Marie Fortune, right?" a woman asked as he she walked rather dramatically to their table. Marie hadn't seen her approaching, so she had no idea if she had already been in the diner, or if she had just come in, saw her, and singled her out. Whatever the case, the tone of her simple question made it quite clear that she was not a happy camper.

"Yes, I'm Marie. Can I help you?"

"You don't know who I am, do you?" she asked.

Marie studied the woman's face for a moment. The lady's features were tightly drawn due to the anger. She was a very pretty woman that looked to be close to her age, maybe a few years younger. She had a well-trimmed body and brown eyes that seemed to be both plain and overly expressive all at the same time. Marie was pretty confident she had never met this woman before in her life.

"I'm sorry but no, I don't think I do," Marie said

"My name is Katie Stillson," the woman said. "And I want to know just how on earth you managed to sabotage my inn!"

CHAPTER FIVE

It took a few moments for the name to ring a bell and when it did, that bell became more like fire sirens, screeching in her mind. How many times had she heard Posey mention a woman named Katie Stillson? How many times had her name come up whenever June Manor's troubles reared their head? Yes, Marie knew the name well, but had never met the woman.

"Katie Stillson," Marie said. "The owner of Shoreline Oaks."

"That right," Katie said quite loudly. Her hands were on her hips and she was staring down at Marie as if waiting for some sort of response. "And I want to know—"

"I heard you the first time," Marie snapped. "There's no need to be loud about it. If you want to speak to me about something, we can do it outside."

"Oh yeah, I'm sure you'd prefer that," Katie said. "Lord knows your reputation is already on the skids around here."

"No," Marie said, noticing that at least a dozen people had turned and started staring at them. "I just think it's terribly rude to get into a shouting match while people are trying to eat."

"Well, if you—" Katie started, but this time she was interrupted by Abagail.

"Stop trying to start a scene," Abagail told her. "She already said she'll talk with you outside. So go. Talk. Don't make an ass of yourself, dear."

The comment shocked Katie, but the shock was muted by the oddly sweet way in which her mother had taken up for her. For all she knew, it was the first time that had happened over the course of her life. Marie took advantage of Katie's own feigned shock by getting to her feet and starting for the door. When she did, her shoulder bumped Katie's and she cringed. She'd not done it intentionally and was sure a woman that flew off the handle like Katie might see it as a sign of aggression. But she made it outside without any further incident. She opened the door and before it even had a chance to close behind her, Katie was there.

Marie noted that her mother had elected to stay inside—for which Marie was very grateful.

"So how did you do it?" Katie asked.

"Do what, exactly?" Marie asked. She was still a little too confused to be properly angry but she was quickly getting there.

"You know exactly what I'm talking about! You…you…you've managed to somehow haunt my inn!"

"Haunt…are you…what?" Marie felt about a thousand words trying to come out all at once and then managed to control herself. She took a deep breath and then tried again. "Even if I *wanted* to sabotage your inn, I could not haunt it," she said. "In order to haunt a place, I'd have to be dead. And as you can see…well, I'm clearly not dead."

"Oh, you know what I mean!" Katie said. She looked so furious that Marie thought the woman was going to stomp her feet and start throwing a tantrum.

"But I assure you, I *don't."* Marie insisted.

"Shoreline Oaks is haunted," Katie said. Her voice was quite loud as she said *haunted,* she lowered her volume and looked around quickly as if making sure no one had heard her say it. "My inn is haunted and it wasn't a few days ago. Everything was fine and then *bam!* All of a sudden, there's a ghost. And a mean one at that!"

"And you think…what?" Marie asked. "Do you seriously think I had something to do with it?"

"Well, not's play stupid here," Katie said, folding her arms and leering at Marie. "I know about your reputation. Everyone in Port Bliss knows about it, for that matter. Who else in town would be able to cause a place to be haunted?"

"Again," Marie said. "It really seems like you don't understand how a haunting works."

"I saw your comments on Facebook," Katie said. "You think I missed that?"

"Facebook? What are you—"

But then she did remember losing her temper right around Halloween, when Shoreline Oaks had really been pressing hard to make June Manor look bad. In one of Katie's Facebook posts where she'd been bad-mouthing June Manor and throwing soft accusations at Marie, Marie had made some sort of silly comment. Something about "be careful how you talk about us or we'll send our ghosts after you…"

"Are you serious?" Marie said. "That one comment I made about ghosts right around Halloween?"

"That's right!"

"So not only do you not know how hauntings work, but apparently you have no idea how jokes work, either."

"You can insult me all you want, but—"

"These aren't insults," Marie said, the anger starting to finally come to the surface now. "These are facts. I was joking when I left that comment. I don't know what you've heard about me, but I'm not some sort of witch that can send spirits to haunt places. That's just ridiculous."

"So…what? You expect me to think that my otherwise perfect inn just all of a sudden got a resident ghost?"

Marie understood a few things in that moment. First of all, while Katie Stillson was indeed very angry, the root of that anger was based in fear. Second, there were still a lot of people watching them from inside Red Reef, including her mother. There were a few people on the streets craning their neck to get a good look at the argument as well. *Just what I need,* Marie thought. *To be the center of another public dispute.*

"Look," Marie said. "There is absolutely no way you can prove I did this, nor can I prove I did not."

"Oh, I'm sure you did it," Katie said. "I just know it. I know…"

"Katie, listen to me. I've learned enough about this stuff over the last several months to have at least some sort of grasp on how it works. I'm sure there are at least some edges to the rumors you've heard that are true. And I can assure you, I do not have the power to send a ghost to someone else's property to haunt it. That's absurd." Then, as an afterthought, she asked: "Are you even certain there's a ghost?"

The anger in Katie's face softened a bit. She also started looking around at their surroundings and realized she had created quite a scene. "Yes," she said. And with that single word, it was almost as if she'd made the transition from enemy to confidante. "I've seen things moving by themselves…pictures flying off the walls, plates and bowls slamming against the walls. Just before the holidays I had a guest report someone shoving them down the stairs but there was no one else upstairs. The latest thing occurred just last night, when a guest woke up to their bed being shaken. Knocked him right out of bed."

Marie suddenly felt very cold and she knew it had very little to do with the blustery winter weather they were currently standing in. "Katie…I need you to level with me. Are you being serious?"

"Yes, I'm being serious!"

"So it's not just seeing things here and there and people being spooked? Things are breaking and people are being harmed?"

"Yes," she said, looking very worried and scared herself.

"Then this needs to stop," Marie said. "This is more than a ghost. This sounds more like some sort of—"

"A poltergeist," Katie finished for her. "I know. I looked it up."

It was a real enough threat in Marie's eyes to allow whatever rift had formed between them to be looked past. "If you'd like, I can see what I can do. I could come by and—"

"No, I don't think so," Katie said. Some of the venom started to rise back into her voice and the anger swiftly took front and center again. "There's no way I'm letting you in my house to bring in more of your nonsense!"

"Katie, I've never even been in your damned house!"

Now it was Marie that was screaming and she knew that needed to be the end of the conversation. She held her hands up in defeat and shook her head. "I'm going to back inside and finish having hot chocolate and pie with my mother. If you follow me, I'll ask the owner to call the police on you for harassment."

Katie gave her a knowing little grin and said, "Oh yeah…you and Robbie right? I'm sure he'd call the police. I'm sure he'd do just about anything you ask." Seeing Marie's look of embarrassment and shock, Katie added: "There are more than just ghostly rumors going around about you, you know."

And with that, Katie Stillson turned on her heel and started walking away. Marie watched for just a moment before heading back inside where she didn't think even the amazing hot chocolate was going to be able to get rid of the chill that continued to make its way through her.

When she made her way back inside, all eyes were on her for a moment and then drifted slowly away. Robbie was among them and she went to reclaim her seat, he walked up to her and spoke quietly.

"What was that about?" he asked.

"I'd like to say it was nothing but some friendly competition, but that would be a lie. She thinks I…well, it's a bit much. I really don't want to get into it."

"Oh," was all he said. His eyes looked downward and Marie realized it was the first time in a while that she had chosen not to share her troubles and struggles with him. Apparently, he noticed it, too. He gave her a little nod and headed back behind the counter.

Feeling embarrassed and a little sad, Marie slid back into the booth. She felt her mother's eyes on her without actually having to see it.

"You okay?" Abagail asked.

"Yeah, it's fine."

"That woman…she seemed crazy. You know her?"

"Not well," Marie said, still finding it hard to look up at her mother. "But I'm afraid I'm probably going to have to sooner rather than later."

CHAPTER SIX

The following morning, Marie woke up with a sudden thought in her head. It was not a thought that had the chance to present itself yesterday because it had been mostly blocked by the uncharacteristic anger she'd felt toward Katie Stillson. But with a refreshed mind, the thought popped into her head immediately upon waking and Marie could not let it go.

Katie seemed very scared yesterday. Has she believed in ghosts all along, or was it a belief spurred on by her recent events?

Marie wasn't quite sure why, but it felt like a very important question. In the social medial blasts Shoreline Oaks had been putting out against June Manor, Katie had always made a point to take light (and sometimes not-so-light jabs) at Marie's inadvertent ties to the paranormal community. And having wrestled with her own disbelief and feelings on the paranormal, Marie couldn't help but wonder…was Katie more scared of the potential poltergeist in her inn, or of what it might do to her business and reputation?

When Marie made it downstairs for the morning's first cup of coffee, she found Posey, Rebeka, and her mother sitting at the dining room table. There would be no guests at June Manor until January 2nd—not anything Marie had planned; the week after Christmas was apparently just not a good week for bed and breakfasts. The three women were all laughing about something and moods seemed to be great. And who could blame them? The house smelled of Posey's typical hearty breakfast: sausage and bacon, omelets and fresh biscuits. When Posey saw her, she smiled widely and waved to her.

"Get your coffee and meet me in the sitting room," Posey said. "There's something you need to filled in on."

"That's not the way I was hoping to start my day," Marie said cautiously.

"No, no, this is good."

Marie nodded, noting that even her mother seemed to be in good spirits. As Marie poured her coffee, Abagail was chatting with another woman about gardening—a topic Marie had no idea her mother was interested in. She supposed she was going to have to spend a lot more time with her mother to truly catch up and learn all of the smaller details of her life. It may take some time, though; she was still reeling from the news that her mother had the same gift she did, only apparently it was supercharged and had pointed her towards a thirty year journey for answers.

She gave her mother a smile of acknowledgement as she excused herself into the sitting room with Posey. Posey was standing anxiously in the center of the room and she had a look on her face that Marie was coming to think of as Posey's mischievous expression.

"Posey, what have you done?" she asked with a smile.

"For once, this is not my doing," she said, working quickly to pull up something on her phone. "But remember how you told me about your hostile run-in with Katie Stillson yesterday?"

"I thought you said this was a good thing," Marie said.

"Oh, it is," Posey said, showing Marie that she had pulled up the Shoreline Oaks Facebook page on her phone. "It seems she went looking for sympathy and to get people on her side and it's starting to backfire."

Marie looked at the posts Posey had scrolled to. In one of them, Katie Stillson had taken a pretty big gamble and gone public with the frightening rumors that had already started circulating about Shoreline Oaks. Late yesterday evening, Katie posted:

"I prefer to get in front of these sorts of things, so I will go ahead and admit it right now: yes, the rumors appear to be true. In keeping with some of the rich history of our coast, it seems that Shoreline Oaks has its very own supernatural resident. But rather than try hiding these stories (like some other B and B owners in the area) I wanted to show my public and potential guests the respect they deserve. Spooky residents or not, Shoreline Oaks will always be here for the community and those from out of town that want to know more about Port Bliss and the surrounding areas."

Marie's first reaction was anger, but it was quickly replaced with confusion. Just yesterday, Katie had seemed legitimately terrified as she'd explained the things happening at her inn. And then, in a post written not even ten hours later, she was using it as a way to make herself look better. But before she could get too carried away, she looked to the comments beneath the post and saw what Posey was talking about. There were twenty-three comments so far and they were surprising to say the least.

One woman stated: "Yeah, but weren't you mocking that 'other B and B owner in the area' for the same thing just a few weeks ago?"

A man a few comments below that one stated: "Does no one have original ideas anymore? Shame on you, copycat."

A third comment said: "June Manor opens, then out of nowhere, you open. June Manor is rumored to be somehow associated with haunting and ghosts, and now somehow so is your place? You expect us to believe that? Doesn't seem like you 'respect' us at all!"

There were a few comments that applauded Katie's bravery, from former guests and locals that vowed to continue to support her. For each of those comments, someone else had responded to those comments with a suggestion to check out June Manor next time. Marie was rather proud to find that several of the people posting in her favor were people that had stayed at June Manor in the past.

"They're being pretty brutal, huh?" Marie said, hanging the phone back to her. Honestly, she wasn't quite sure how to feel about it.

"They are," Posey said. "But I do believe that's what you call a backfire. Maybe now she'll just run her own business and stop trying to run other people through the mud."

"Maybe," Marie said, and then took a sip of her coffee. "But you know…I think she might actually have a ghost issue. When she was describing it to me yesterday, I don't think she was messing around. She looked really scared."

Posey sighed at the show of kindness—kindness Marie assumed seemed very naïve. "Well," she said snidely. "Serves her right if you ask me. Take a look at the post she made below that one…"

Marie had to read it twice just to make sure she was reading it correctly. The woman was either losing her mind, or getting desperate to save face after having been so thoroughly whipped in her previous post.

"I did not intend for this to become a me vs. someone else issue. However, based on things I've heard, I also don't think it's outside the realm of possibility that the things currently taking place in Shoreline Oaks were caused and staged by a certain SOMEONE that you all keep referring to."

The comments that followed this consisted of things like "Outrageous!" and "You've lost your marbles!" and lots of eye-roll emojis.

And still, Marie felt that the core of it all was fear. Katie Stillson may have originally opened her bed and breakfast as some sort of competition for June Manor for spiteful reasons Marie did not fully understand. But now that she'd more or less established herself as an equally thriving business, she was having issues that were beyond any logical human's ability to understand. If she was indeed dealing with a poltergeist, Marie assumed most of her reactions online, as well as her reaction to Marie at Red Reef, had all been fear-based. And honestly, Marie felt sorry for her.

"I think this might spell the end of Katie Stillson," Posey said.

"Maybe," Marie said.

"I thought you'd be relieved."

"A part of me is, for sure," Marie said. "But like I said…I saw how bothered she was when she yelled at me yesterday. I saw…I don't know. She's scared, Posey. She's scared and isn't handling it the best way."

Posey, seeing that she wasn't going to get Marie on the same celebratory level that she was on, nodded. She pocketed her phone and headed back into the dining room almost like a dog with its tail tucked between its legs. Marie thought about calling out to her to better explain herself but decided not to. It was too early in the morning for this sort of contemplation and possible drama. So instead, she simply returned to the dining room where the sound of her mother's laughter seemed to call out to her over a barren field of thirty years.

***

She was working up a simple New Year's ad for social media, offering new guests a fifteen percent New Year's discount, when there was a knock on her front door. Marie was sitting at the little check-in station in the foyer when the knock came, and she looked to the door. From her time as a bed and breakfast owner, she'd come to understand that a knock on the door was rather unnatural. People that had paid to be guests rarely knocked—they just came right in. And besides…she wasn't expecting any new guests for another four days. Curious, Marie stepped away from her little workstation and walked to the door.

When she answered it, she found a rather tall woman dressed in a fancy winter coat waiting on the other side. Her black hair was done up in lazy-looking curls and her pretty, angular face was reddened by the cold. She had a sort of '50s era actress look to her and when she smiled, it seemed one hundred percent genuine. She looked to be fifty years old or so, but her smile made her look much younger.

"Can I help you?" Marie asked.

"You're Marie Fortune, correct?" the woman asked.

"Guilty. And you are?"

The smile faltered a bit but then regained its strength. The woman held out a well- manicured hand and said: "Eva Blake. Good to meet you. Can I come in and have a chat?"

"Of course," Marie said, a little confused and bowled over. There was nothing intimidating about Eva Blake but she had the sort of aura about her that seemed to make people instantly want to please her.

Eva came in and instantly started eyeing the place. The smile remained on her face and stretched even wider. No sooner had she closed the door than Boo appeared. He circled her once and then sat down, looking up at her as if looking for approval. Apparently, her odd charm worked on dogs, too. When she leaned down and scratched his head without much effort, it got Boo's tail wagging instantly.

"This place is just as gorgeous as I imagined it," Eva said. She shrugged out of her fancy coat to reveal a very elegant button-down black shirt. It looked like a blend of something out of a Harlequin romance, but updated.

"What is it, exactly, that you wanted to chat about?" Marie asked. "And I mean no disrespect at all by this, but...should I know who you are or why you're here?"

"I'd rather hoped the name would have rung a bell or two," Eva said. As she ventured into the sitting room, still looking around like a kid at an amusement park, she finally got around to explaining herself. "I've written several books about the paranormal and psychology. Books about how the two sort of go hand-in-hand in many cases—and how the paranormal can be explained away by certain psychological theories. Ironically enough, they do much better in the supernatural field. Several days ago, my agent was contacted by a local woman about coming out to do a study at her home. Originally, I was going to say no but then I recalled that the town of Port Bliss sounded familiar. And it sounded familiar because I had read many articles about you earlier this year—about you, your bed and breakfast, and some supposed abilities that you might have."

"Wait…so you know who I am?" Marie asked, a bit flummoxed.

"Of course. My area of expertise requires that I stay in the know about paranormal and supernatural news, though most if it is garbage. For a while there, you were a hot topic in the really dedicated circles. Were you not aware?"

"Oh, no, I was aware. It just…I don't know. I thought it had died out."

"Dear, people in the paranormal community cling to *anything.* It's part of their gullibility. Anything that might one day resurface to be newsworthy is held in high regard. Between you and me," she said, lowering her voice even though there was no one else in the room, "it's the main reasons my books sell so well."

Marie considered herself a patient person, but she was quickly starting to not care for the way Eva Blake seemed to look down on those in the paranormal community. "Well, I hope meeting me isn't the main reason you decided to come to Port Bliss," Marie said.

"It just made the decision easier. It also helped that this area of the state seems to be rich in ghostly folklore. Anyway…you and I can talk about your experiences later, if that's okay with you. First, though, I supposed I should get right down to business."

"And what business is that?"

"The woman that contacted my agent…the one that requested I perform a study at her business. She—"

"My God," Marie said. "Is her name Katie Stillson, by any chance?"

"Why yes," Eva said with that same bright smile. "You know her?"

Marie sighed and said: "Maybe a little too well. And it seems I severely underestimated her."

"Whatever do you mean?" Eva asked.

Marie folded her arms over her chest and started pacing as the anger that had introduced itself yesterday in front of the Red Reef Diner came back in full swing. "Have a seat, Mrs. Blake," she said. "This could take a while and—"

She was interrupted by yet another knock at the door. She was almost annoyed by the sound this time. She walked quickly to it, wondering who else might be coming by to gauge her opinions of Katie

Stillson and Shoreline Oaks. What other surprises were going to be tossed in her face due to Katie's little act?

She opened the door, doing her best to keep her anger at bay. But what she saw on the other side not only pushed the anger away…it obliterated it into tiny little specks that were blown away by the sheer surprise of it all.

She looked to the person on the other side of the door and had to force the words out of her mouth. She was dizzy for a moment and her heart slammed in her chest as she spoke her next two words.

"Hey, Brendan."

CHAPTER SEVEN

They stood on opposite sides of the doorway for three seconds before anyone said anything. As Marie searched for words, she studied him intently. Had his brown eyes always been that penetrating? Had he always been this handsome? Did the corners of that crooked smile always seem so well-defined?

You know you're staring, right? some scared voice inside said.

Brendan finally responded with a rather uninspired: "Hey yourself. Is this a bad time?"

"Why would you ask that?" she said. Oh, how she hated that it was far too hard not to attack him with a hug. She felt herself literally having to keep her arms pinned to her side.

"You look flustered," he said. "And I see that the new additions are done," he added, looking over to his right. "I figure you must be really busy."

"No, not a bad time," she said. "Just a weird time. I can't…hold on. What are you even doing here?"

"It's a funny story, actually," he said. He then peered into the doorway and said: "So…can I come in and tell you?"

"My gosh, yes, of course," she stammered, embarrassed that she had not yet invited him inside. "Come on in."

Brendan stepped forward and made it no further inside before Boo came charging at him. Brendan looked just as excited to see Boo as the other way around and it was both heartwarming and a little silly to watch their reunion. She also wished she could show how happy she was to see Brendan with the same freedom and excitement as her dog. She closed the door and started walking towards the sitting room, wondering just how strange the round of introductions she was about to make would be.

She was actually rather glad Eva Blake had arrived five minutes before Brendan because it gave her a tangible reason to not stare at Brendan. In all reality, it had been less than a month since they'd last seen one another, but it felt like much longer. She turned to Eva and gave her a grin that seemed to say *boys will be boys.*

“Sorry, Mrs. Blake,” she said as Boo and Brendan finished up their hellos. “This is my good friend B—”

“My God, it’s Brendan Peck,” Eva said. Her eyes were wide and the smile on her face had somehow managed to grow even wider.

Brendan finally looked up from Boo and though his eyes first settled warmly on Marie, they then ventured to the older woman that had spoken his name. A little glimmer of recognition sparkled in his eyes and he stepped forward extending his hand.

“Eva Blake,” he said. “Nice to see you again.”

They shook heartily, with the excitement of two people that truly were happy to see one another.

“I guess I won’t even pretend to be surprised that the two of you know one another,” Marie said. There was no ill will in the statement, but a tone of someone that has been invited to the party but feels left out.

“Oh, Mr. Peck and I have something of an everlasting debate going on,” Eva said rather proudly.

“We run into each other a lot at conferences,” Brendan explained. “We’ve spent a lot of time at bars bickering back and forth about the psychological ramifications of paranormal activity.”

“And while we disagree most of the time,” Eva said, “he was nice enough to provide a blurb for my last book. It was even a very positive one, at that.”

“It was a good book,” Brendan said. “Even if I *did* disagree with most of it.”

Now Marie was *really* starting to not like Eva. But this was mostly out of jealousy. “Okay, so Mrs. Blake, at the risk of seeming rude,” Marie said, “I sort of need to speak with Brendan in private. I wasn’t expecting him and we—”

“That’s right!” Eva said, giving a solitary clap of her hands in excitement. “I seem to recall Brendan’s name popping up in the articles I read about you. He thought he had undeniable proof of a haunting here, isn’t that right?”

“Yes, I thought I did,” Brendan said. He locked eyes with Marie and smiled. “It turned out okay, though. It’s a very long story.”

“Well, then,” Eva said, apparently forgetting that Marie had done her best to have a private word with Brendan no more than five seconds ago. “During your time here in Port Bliss, did you happen to encounter a woman by the name of Katie Stillson?”

"Not physically, but I knew her by name." He again gave Marie a little smile here and then, with a puzzled look on his face, he said: "That *is* why I'm in town, though. Did she contact you, too?"

"She did," Eva said with a nod.

It all seemed to gather up in Marie's head in a single instant and exploded into sudden realization. "Oh…wait just a second. Are you telling me that Katie Stillson reached out to *both* of you about this alleged haunting at her place?"

"Seems that way," Brendan said. It was apparent he wanted to say much more but was hesitant to do so in front of Eva. Marie found herself wanting Eva to take a hike quite badly.

"She contacted my agent the day after Christmas," Eva said. "She seemed very genuine and scared."

"I got an email and then I called her," Brendan said. "Because of how I'd heard of her in the past, trying to mess with June Manor's success, I was skeptical. But I agree with Eva. Katie sounded genuinely upset. I can smell a fraud pretty good, and I think she's for real."

"You don't think it's a trap?" Marie asked. "Come on, Brendan. If she was so set against June Manor and my success, surely she knew about our…well, our *history*. She could be just doing it to mess with me."

"I considered that," Brendan said. "But I really don't think that's the case here. Or, if it is, it's not the *entire* case."

"Ah," Eva said, looking back and forth between them as if she were watching a tennis match. "So you two used to…?"

"It's complicated," Brendan said. Marie found that his eyes kept coming back to her and it made her feel special. It made her remember how much she'd liked having him around—how her heart would soar when he made it back to Port Bliss between conferences and ghost hunts.

"Okay, so here's what I propose," Marie said. She hated that she was so irritated; there was too much going on all at once. Not only that, but none of this had even been an issue fifteen minutes ago. Way back then, her life had been about as normal as it could get…unexpectedly having her mother as a guest aside. "Brendan and I need to have a talk in private. Before that, though, I would really like to know what's going on with both of you and Katie Stillson."

"Well, as I told you," Eva said. "She's asked me to come have a look around. She admitted to me that she had no idea who I was until about two weeks ago. Since then, when her haunting started, she's read all of my books. She likes my approach and skepticism. I sort of got the idea that she hopes I can come up with some answer other than 'your house is haunted.'"

"And as for me, the new show isn't out yet but people in the paranormal community are already talking about it. She admitted that she did a Google search for *ghost expert* and my name was the first that popped up. I know she's not truthful about *that.* The first guy that pops up is this genius out of New Orleans, but he charges ten grand just to come visit. I'm the first one she got to that doesn't charge an arm and a leg. And I guess my face being all over forums and Facebook helped."

"So she wants both of you to document it?" Marie asked.

"More or less," Brendan asked. "Let's be real here…I considered not coming. Just because…well, you know. *Us.* But my producer had a great point. I have ties to Port Bliss now. And people *do* connect you and I bit now. So it was a no-brainer. It's sort of the perfect set-up for the show."

"Oh, I see." So he hadn't come with any sort of desire to see her after all. Apparently it was indeed all business.

He apparently saw the hurt on her face because he finally looked to Eva and, rather rudely, said: "Sorry, but could you excuse us?"

Eva nodded, giving them both a smile as Brendan started walking away. Marie felt odd following him through her own house. They walked out onto the back patio and it seemed that Brendan regretted it at once. He winced at the cold and shook his head.

"This right here," he said, "is about the only thing I like *more* about LA. Everything else is just too damned busy."

"If you're cold, why not just say what you need to say?" Marie asked.

"Well, first and foremost, seeing you made the last few weeks confirm one thing for me. I knew I missed you, but I thought I was sort of being dramatic about it. But that's not true at all. It's so good to see you again."

"I'd say the same," she said, trying to stay in control of her emotions. "But based on everything you said in there, it seems you're only back to appease Katie Stillson and your network."

"Those *are* both reasons I came back. But they aren't the only ones. I almost said no. I almost stayed in LA and pissed my producer *and* the network off. You made it clear that you and I weren't going to work and I didn't think it would be a good idea. And then when I was basically pushed into it, I told myself that I wouldn't come see you because I wasn't sure if you'd want me to. But then I figured you'd hear from someone—Posey, probably—that I had been in town and…I don't know. I didn't want to take the chance that you'd be hurt."

That said, he looked out to the ocean. His arms were crossed against his chest, trying to keep warm. She wanted to kiss him but didn't dare do it. After all, she was the one that ended things. What sort of message would that be sending?

"For what it's worth," she said, "I'm glad you decided to come. I've missed you, too. And I'm sorry about my reaction in there, but Katie Stillson and I had a little run-in yesterday. She's trying to accuse me of causing her house to be haunted."

"Did you explain to her that's not exactly how hauntings work?"

"Yes, I tried quite hard. But it reminded me about this little vendetta she has against me—for reasons I am still not clear on. And if it turns out she's just trying to use you to get at me somehow, I'm going to likely end up in prison."

"Ooh, and you would not do well in prison," he joked. "Okay…so now that all of that is cleared up, can we get back inside? I'm freaking freezing out here."

"Yeah," she said. She hesitated a moment, again fighting the reaction to kiss him, to just give him a hug. She instead walked quickly to the back door and they walked back inside. As they did, she noted that in the small amount of time they'd spent outside, another person had showed up in the sitting room.

Her mother had come back from town and was already chatting with Eva Blake. It seemed her mother knew exactly who Eva was and was thrilled to meet her. And when her eyes landed on Brendan and grew wide, it was apparent that she knew who he was, too.

June Manor was getting quite full and Marie could not remember the last time she'd felt so much tension and awkwardness. And given the way her life had gone over the past year, that was saying a hell of a lot.

CHAPTER EIGHT

As it turned out, things weren't quite as awkward as Marie feared they might be—and it was all because of Posey and Rebeka.

Within ten minutes of the unexpected foursome occupying the sitting room, Posey and Rebeka came out with tea and charcuterie board that had been thrown together quickly but was still quite impressive. It was all set before them on the coffee table and what happened next was, in Marie's estimation, the absolute strangest and most vulnerable conversation she'd ever been a part of. Boo also made sure to be at the center of it, sniffing around floor along the edges of the coffee table just in case any crumbs made their way to the rug.

"I suppose my main concern," Eva said, "is that Katie Stillson might be trying to use my name as something of a marketing ploy. I don't doubt she's scared and there might be legitimate activity there, but her intent behind it all is what I am calling into question."

"Well, when is the so-called investigation supposed to take place?" Marie asked, nibbling on crackers and cheese.

"Tonight for me," Eva said.

"Same here," Brendan responded. "And if you put that all together—having people like me and Eva out there at the same time—it does start to seem like more marketing than anything else."

"Forgive me," Abagail said. "I'm still sort of caught up in the excitement of it all. I've read all of your books, Mrs. Blake and I've obviously seen you on television, Mr. Peck. Maybe we can all reconnect later and I'll tell you all about my own supernatural journeys."

"Journeys?" Brendan asked.

"Yeah, about that," Marie said. "It seems my little talent is sort of a biological thing. Mom has it, too."

"What? I don't even...how can..." He stopped here, laughing out loud at the absurdity of it all. He finally caught up to himself and took a deep breath. "One thing at a time, though. I'm sorry, Ms. Fortune...you were saying?"

She grinned at him and continued: "I was just saying…for now, as a mother, I have to ask myself the most important question: why does Katie Stillson seem to have something against Marie in the first place?"

"I have no idea," Marie said. "At first I thought it was just her trying to be competitive because we run similar businesses. But this whole thing with her trying to blame this alleged haunting on me takes it to another level."

"And *that's* why I think there might be something to the haunting," Brendan said. "She's desperate, throwing around accusations like that. Even if it *does* potentially make you look bad, she has to know it's going to make her sound like a nutcase, too."

"Hold on a moment," Eva said, looking pointedly at Abagail. "I want to know more about these supernatural journeys Mrs. Fortune has been on. Surely if she had some sort of link to the supernatural and Marie does as well, is there something there we need to explore?"

"With the utmost respect, I'd rather not," Abagail said. "There are things I still need to tell Marie before I reveal it to strangers—personal things that I am still processing."

"Yeah, same here," Marie said, looking at her mother with a sort of appreciation that didn't quite make sense to her.

"Well, tell me, Marie," Eva said. "I've read a few articles about what may or may not have happened in this home and no one has ever quite properly laid out the talents that you possess. Would you mind telling me about them?"

At first, Marie was going to decline. Brendan already knew most of the details about her so-called talents and there was something almost intimate about that. But she also knew that sharing it out loud with someone like her mother might actually do her some good. She had more or less come to terms that she had this odd gift (a gift she still did not quite understand) and had accepted it as a part of her. Looking at her mother, Brendan, and Eva, she felt at peace about that part of her for the first time in…well, maybe ever. Brendan had always managed to make her feel comfortable with it, but she'd always fought against it. Maybe it was being in the presence of three people that all believed in and respected what she had been wrestling with that simply made it easier.

"I'm still not one hundred percent sure how it works," she said. "I mean, have no doubt that I'm able to see ghosts more than the usual person. I think I might actually be able to sort of sense them before they appear. But it's more than that. I can sort of feel what they're feeling. And when I encounter ones that appear to be malevolent, I get this sort of…I don't know. There's this rage that comes out of me and I literally just scream at them."

"Like, cursing them out?" Eva asked.

"No. Just screaming. It's like this primal reaction. And so far, every time I've done this, the spirit just sort of disappears and is never seen or heard from again."

"That's…odd," Abagail said, though there was no doubt or ridicule in it. It seemed like she wanted to say something else but was trying to hold it back—perhaps for a more opportune time, Marie wondered if it was one of those things she'd said she wanted to share with her in private.

"So then it seems to me that if Katie does have a poltergeist in her place, you'd be a pretty useful tool," Brendan said. "Also, you know…you'd sort of get an inside glimpse at her operations."

"We're not playing Spy vs. Spy here," Marie said. "And I doubt she'd just invite me over."

"You won't need to," Brendan said. "I'll insist that I want your expertise on my side. Well, yours and your sidekick, of course."

"Sidekick?" Eva asked.

"Yeah, that's where it gets a little weirder," Marie said. "I don't quite understand the connection just yet, but it seems Boo has a touch of these gifts as well. At first I thought it was all him but…well, it turned out to be mostly me. I don't quite know how it all works, but my powers are sort of amplified when he's around."

"I think I agree with Brendan," Eva said. "If she has a legitimate problem, it seems like you'd be the best person for the job. That is…if she wants the ghost gone. *If* there is a ghost. I told her upfront that I do not come to these things looking for evidence of the supernatural. I come looking for ways to disprove it all—to find a rational explanation."

"Based on what I'm hearing," Marie said, "I don't know that you're going to come out of this happy."

"Whether you believe there's a poltergeist there or not," Marie said, "at the end of the day *she* is going to need to believe that it's gone. As for me, I've seen and experienced these things and I feel like…I don't know. Maybe I'm supposed to be part of it."

"Then come along," Brenda said with an edge of excitement.

"I don't know. Like I said, I don't think she'd be open to the idea."

"Well, let's try it anyway. The worst thing that can happen is that she says no and gets pissy. But on the flip side, maybe you can run this spirit off and she'll drop whatever this vendetta is against you."

Marie shrugged and raised her hands in defeat. She absolutely did not want to help Katie Stillson in any way. But the more they talked it out, the more it made sense that she should be part of it all. Sure, she did not like the woman, but that didn't mean she could sit by and let her be tormented by something potentially evil.

"If it's something you want to pursue, go ahead," Marie said. "And if she'll have me, I'll be there."

Boo had come and settled down between their chairs. He watched them talk, looking back and forth between them. He tended to look at Brendan longer. It was clear that he had missed Brendan and was happy to have him back. *I know the feeling, boy,* Marie thought.

"Speaking of *being there,"* Eva said, "I should probably head over to Shoreline Oaks. She'll be expecting me." She then made a point to look directly at Marie and added: "This conversation stays here. Now, I may fess up to having heard about you through my research and whatnot, but that will be all. And thank you for the time, information, and snacks."

"Of course. And thank you."

Eva went around the room shaking hands and when she made her exit, it seemed as if some energy left the room. She clearly had some sort of pull to her, the sort of woman that brought joy and excitement to any room.

"And as for me," Brendan said when she was gone, "I need to find some place to stay for the next night or so. Would you happen to know anywhere I could stay?"

"You big doofus," she said. She busted out such a sophisticated word because she needed to find some way to hide the excitement of Brendan staying at June Manor again.

They locked eyes for a moment and Marie nearly forgot that her mother was even in the room. This was rectified as Abagail stood up and said, without much tact, "I think I'll go see if I can bug Posey."

Brendan bit back a laugh as Abagail left the room. "So…that's your mother, huh?"

"Yeah. It's been a…well, it's been an interesting week. And today is just the topping on the cake."

"So…your mom is in town and you get to see her for the first time in about thirty years *and* you have this stuff going on with Katie Stillson. And you're dealing with the discovery that your mother also has a little bit of the spooky to her. You sure it's okay if I stay here?"

"Of course," she said.

"Any new room or ghosts or curses or anything I need to know about?"

"No, don't be stu—oh, wait. Yes, there is. I haven't told you about the secret underground room yet, have I?"

Brendan finally let the laugh out and when he reached out and took her hand playfully, she didn't stop him. "The fact that I can't tell if you're being serious or messing with me is one of the many reasons I've missed you so much."

"So, do you want to see it?"

"A secret underground room? Um…of course I do."

She took him by the hand as if they were middle schoolers about to cross the playground and led him to the basement door. And on the way, she did not even mind the little look of amusement both Posey and her mother gave her from the kitchen. She opened the basement door and led Brendan down the stairs to let him in on even more of her secrets.

***

"So, are you going to tell me willingly, or am I going to have to pull it out of you?" Abagail asked.

Marie looked up from her laptop and saw her mother standing in the entryway between the foyer and the sitting room. She'd been looking ahead at bookings for January; she wasn't packed by any means but had a respectable number of guests coming in.

"Pull what out of me?" Marie asked, though she was pretty sure she knew.

"About the C-list celebrity you just booked in an upstairs room of your bed and breakfast. I don't know if *you* saw it, but he had a very hard time keeping his eyes off of you."

"I'm not sure we're there yet, Mom. Even I don't quite know all of the details about why we didn't work out. Aside from his going to LA and me being here, with a brand new business to take care of…"

"So you *did* date?"

"We did. Sort of. And that's about as much information as you're going to get out of me until I get more details about your trip."

Abagail grinned and came over to the check-in desk. "Well, I spent all that time looking for answers and it seems that back home, my daughter had some of those same questions. And if I'm being honest with you, there was one moment about twelve years ago when I did almost come looking for you. I'd met with a man in Nepal that could communicate with the dead—sort of a psychic I guess, but for ghosts. He had a theory that it's all in the bloodline. If the mother has it, the daughter will have it. But sometimes it takes a sort of vessel to help the gift stay contained to that bloodline."

"Vessel?"

"Yes. Anything that contains people and their lives—their essence. Something," she said, gesturing all around them, "like a house. I did some research on it and there are many spiritual people in the East that buy into it. And if you really study some of the most famous hauntings in America, there are threads of it there, too."

"So you think June Manor is what…like a conduit for my supernatural abilities?"

"I do. Yours, mine, June's. Maybe even your dog's."

Marie considered this for a moment and it seemed a little too big to properly digest. Still, she felt there might be something there. With a deep sigh, she said, "Well, if that's true, it certainly would answer some long-standing questions. But…did it start with June? Was she the first in our family to have it?"

Abagail shook her head and a rather serious look crept over her face. "No. Some of what I found during my time away was that this goes back pretty far for us. I know for sure it goes back at least three generations, but then I couldn't turn anything else up. And in that second generation, I was able to find deeds to the land June Manor is built on."

"That's…well, that's incredible, Mom. But why are you waiting until now, almost two days after you arrived, to tell me this?"

"Because I had to be sure. I had to first of all be certain that you not only had the gift, but that you were comfortable with it. And then I had to sort of check back in with the house. I don't know if you've picked up on it or not, but it sort of talks, you know? I needed to reorient myself to it."

"And have you?" Marie asked.

"I have." She smiled a bit and then looked up the staircase and then out to the new additions. "It seems happy to have me back. And it feels…I don't know…*proud.* I think if a house has a spirit of its own, you've improved June Manor's with those additions."

"This is starting to sound a little New Age-y," Marie said.

"Oh, it is. There are certain elements of it all that I still don't understand myself. But you *did* ask."

"I know I did. I think—"

She stopped at the sound of a door opening somewhere behind her and footsteps coming down the hall. She turned to see Brendan coming down the hallway. He had his cellphone in his hand and he was wearing a thin little smile she had come to know well—a smile she had missed terribly.

"Just got off the phone with Katie Stillson," Brendan said. "She raised a bit of hell when I even mentioned you. But when I broke it down to her the way we discussed—about how you might be the best bet of getting rid of this thing—she came around. She says it's fine that you come with me tonight."

"Wow. I was *truly* not expecting that."

"It makes me have to play Devil's advocate one more time," Brendan said. "If she's willing to let you come, it has to mean this isn't all a marketing tactic."

"Yeah, I guess not," Marie said. She was not only confused but also suddenly scared. She had casually just gotten involved in what was starting to sound like a pretty terrifying experience. While the idea of Brendan being there with her, she was also much more aware of how intense these situations could be. Her last ghost-busting assignment at the Rock Ridge Hotel had proved that beyond a shadow of a doubt.

"You okay?" Brendan asked.

"I think so," she said, snapping out of it. "I just realized that I sort of volunteered for a case I have no clue about."

"You'll be fine," he said. He gave her a wink and said, "I also got permission for Boo to come. With the two of us, Boo, and Eva Clark coming, that ghost doesn't stand a chance."

Brendan the headed back to his room. Marie was not at all surprised to see Boo following close behind him. When Marie turned back to her mother, she was smiling widely. "Okay…I told you some of my secrets. Now tell me about that," she said cutting her eyes in Brendan's direction.

“Mother, have you always been this insufferable?”

“You know, I like to think I have,” Abagail said with a smile.

Slowly, Marie started to quietly tell her other about the rocky sort of history she and Brendan shared. And though it did lift her spirits a bit to go back over it and realize that he had indeed cared for her, the uncertainty of tonight was lurking at the back of her mind.

CHAPTER NINE

Because of her recent familiarity with all things supernatural, Marie understood why the vast majority of paranormal investigations were conducted at night. There did seem to be a proven theory that most activity occurred after the sun went down—most normally between the hours of midnight and three in the morning. All the same, Marie couldn't help but feel a little cheesy when she and Brendan pulled up in the large driveway of Shoreline Oaks slightly after dusk.

The exterior—from the building itself to the landscaping and surroundings—was gorgeous. Right away, Marie felt a bit of envy nibbling at her. There was a large floodlight positioned about halfway up the large green lawn, highlighting the wraparound porch. There were also small back lights on somewhere at the back of the house and they were positioned just right; they allowed any visitor to catch a breathtaking view of the night surf out on the beach. The house itself was a faint shade of yellow, with all of the trim and decorations painted white. The place looked to be roughly the same size as June Manor, but much more modern. The sidewalk that wound up to the side front steps was bordered in solar lights. A little string of café lights also hung from the left side of the porch, where a cute little sitting area was put together. Due to the cold (*and maybe*, Marie thought, *a lack of guests, too)* there was no one sitting outside tonight.

Brendan parked behind one of the two cars in the driveway and reached for his door. His hand paused for a moment as he looked over to Marie. "Before we go in, I do need to ask you something. And I hope you'll forgive me."

"I'm sure I will," she said, having a pretty good idea where he might be going with it.

From the back seat, Boo poked his head up between them. Apparently, he thought the conversation had something to do with him as well.

"At some point between now and when I leave," Brendan said, "do you think we could *maybe* talk about us?"

“Maybe,” she said, though she wanted to just as badly as he did. She was sure nothing had changed between them as he still had his show and new life in LA and she had June Manor, but maybe there would finally be some well-defined closure. “When *are* you leaving anyway?”

“Well, since this is for the show, they want me to be very thorough with it. There’s tonight’s investigation, and maybe even some additional footage tomorrow night depending on how things go. I told them that I’d rather not travel on New Year’s, so I’m probably in town until at least the second day of January. So about three or four days. That is…if you don’t mind me taking up a room for that long.”

“Hey, you stay as long as you want,” she said. “I’d imagine your hot-shot producers and the network are paying, right?”

In lieu of an answer, Brendan only chuckled. There was a tense moment when they locked eyes over the center console and then he was opening his door and stepping out into the night. Marie followed and assisted with his gear. It felt familiar and somehow fun in a way she had not expected—especially not with the little ball of worry and fear that had nestled deep within her stomach.

Boo leaped out on Brendan’s side and instantly started sniffing at the yard. When he dashed off a little too far along the edge to relieve himself, Marie called him back. They then started for the house, a rather strange-looking trio illuminated harshly by the flood light.

As they made their way to the front porch with all of the gear, another car turned in behind them. Marie recognized the car right away when it parked behind Brendan. She’d spent quite a bit of time driving it around earlier this month. It was Rebeka’s car. And before she had time to wonder why Rebeka would be here, she saw that it was not Rebeka behind the wheel…it was her mother.

“Did you invite her?” Brendan asked.

“I most certainly did not,” Marie said. “She never even asked if she could come along.” She wanted to be angry, but deep down there was a bit of excitement there. She was rather happy that her mother was going to get to see her in action—even if Marie didn’t quite know what to expect herself.

“Ah, so then this will be interesting,” Brendan said. “If you’re good with those bags, I think I’ll head in and let the two of you talk.”

She hefted the two bags she was carrying on her shoulder and said, “Thanks.”

"Good luck," Brendan said as he headed up the stairs. Boo gave Marie an almost apologetic look and then followed after Brendan.

Marie turned toward her mother and cocked her head inquisitively. Abagail frowned and gave a cutesy *I'm sorry* expression.

"What are you doing here, Mom?"

"Well, I had a thought not long after you left…just as you and Brendan headed out the door, in fact. I've spent all that time wandering around the world, looking for answers to this so-called gift. And I really do think there might be more answers here, with you, than anywhere else. And if that's the case, it seems sort of stupid to miss out on the chance to see you at work."

The explanation was a bit confusing and encouraging and Marie wasn't sure how to process it. "So…you're hoping watching me at work might provide you with some sort of answers?"

"That's the hope. I asked Posey if she thought you'd get mad if I came after here and she said she didn't think so. I hate that a stranger knows more about my daughter than me, but…"

"Mom, Posey just loves drama; I love her to death, but she was probably the worst person you could have asked for advice on something like this."

"Yeah, I kind of figured that. It might be why I asked her." She tried a smile that Marie did not return right away. "You want me to go back?"

"No. You're here now. Come on in with me. But if Katie asks you to leave, I don't think we have much leverage in the way of convincing her to let you stay. Me coming was more than enough."

"I can be pretty charming," Abagail said. "It's a trait I passed on to you, or so it seems."

"Flattery will get you nowhere," Marie said, starting for the stairs. "Only in this case, I guess it will. Flattery will get you inside a haunted bed and breakfast."

With a silent little laugh between them, they walked up the stairs and into Shoreline Oaks.

Inside, while the place was absolutely gorgeous and decorated by an obviously trained eye, Marie found the place a little too stuffy. It wasn't the house itself, though; it was the current mood and atmosphere of the place. When Marie and her mother stepped through the front door, the first thing Marie noticed was that Katie had already whisked Brendan away, over to the side where her gorgeous dining room was separated from the massive seating area by nothing more than columns and cornices. She felt like she had stepped into some sort of modern inn rather than a quaint bed and breakfast. The hardwood floors gleamed in the light of the simple yet elegant chandeliers which hung on the very high ceilings.

Before she could make her way over to Katie and Brendan, a small twenty-something woman came hurrying over. She had short, brown hair and a slightly pointed noise that, for some reason, made Marie think she looked a bit like a pixie or fairy.

"Hello," she said, her tone somewhere between sad and angry. She, too, was apparently not a fan of Marie being here. "I'm Sherry Masterson, Katie's assistant. Do you have bags out in the car that need to be brought in?"

"Nope," Marie said. "Just us. No luggage. But thanks for asking."

Sherry Masterson nodded and eyed them both for a moment before leaving. As she watched Sherry leave, Marie and Katie locked eyes over Brendan's shoulder as Katie continued speaking to him. The look of contempt Katie beamed her way felt strong enough to light a fire. Katie also noticed Abagail but seemed to not really care. She turned her attention back to Brendan and spoke quietly as he set his bags down and started looking through them. Boo circled around the bags, sniffed at Katie, and then sat down on the floor like he owned the place.

Marie was not about to give herself a tour, so she simply went to the seating area and sat down. The chairs were quite comfortable, but Marie was too busy trying to decide if they truly looked pretentious or if she was just feeling jealous and protective of her own bed and breakfast. Abagail sat down beside her and looked around slowly.

"This is your competition?" she said.

"Seems that way."

"It feels overdone. Sort of…I don't know…sort of make-believe. It's like a rich little girl got to make a beachside dollhouse. Don't get me wrong; it's absolutely gorgeous. But it feels a bit much, right?"

"I'm glad I'm not the only one who thinks so," Marie said quietly. But she did have to admit it was a beautiful place—like something out of an interior design magazine. She supposed some of her judgement was swayed by the fact that she felt like she was sneaking in behind enemy lines. Or, for a better analogy, maybe she was more like the fly being invited to the spider's web.

When Brendan was done speaking with Katie, he came walking over. Katie hurried off elsewhere, hustling up the wide flight of stairs positioned to the back of the sitting room.

"Everything okay?" Marie asked.

"Yeah. I told her about your mother showing up. She didn't even hesitate. I think she even feels better about *you* being here because she's here."

"Why would that be?" Marie asked.

"I have no idea. I'm starting to understand that Katie Stillson is a very complicated lady. Oh…and you should also know, she's hired one other person to come as well. And between you and me, he's sort of insane."

"Who is it?"

"You ever hear of a dude named Hugh Wrathe?"

"No. But with a name like that, I feel like I should."

"Well, he's on his way. He's a…collector, I suppose? He has this travelling paranormal exhibit. He collects all kinds of paranormal artifacts. He'd be written off as a charlatan and conman if it wasn't for the fact that he just so happens to be an exceptional psychic."

"And why has she invited him?"

"To try to communicate with the ghost."

Abagail spoke up then, uncertain. "Can't that be dangerous?"

"For most people, sure, but Hugh is the real deal. He's also sort of creepy. Just being around him makes you feel odd."

"Great," Marie said. "That'll make tonight much more enjoyable. So where is Eva Blake? How does she feel about this guy coming?"

"Katie says Eva is upstairs in her room. She'll be down in a bit. And I have no idea if she even knows Hugh Wrathe is coming. This feels thrown together…very last minute. And I'm sorry to go there and say it again, but it's even further proof that she's desperate."

"You really think there's something here?" Marie asked.

As if she might be the world's worst spy, the pixie-like Sherry Masterson went walking by. She made no attempt to hide the fact that she was eavesdropping. She stared at each of them as she made her way through the room and then hurried off elsewhere.

"I don't know," Brendan said, placing a perplexed look in the direction of where Sherry had been standing. And then, with a smile, he said, "I think you're the one that should be answering that question. Do *you* feel anything?"

"Other than irritation? No."

"Well, I asked her to not bother with a tour. You know me…I don't like to feel like the host is leading or influencing me. So why don't you and I start the tour?" He then looked over to Abagail and said, "You, too, Mrs. Fortune?"

"Ah, the third wheel," she said.

As they all got up and started for the kitchen area to get a gander at the first floor, the front door came open quickly. The blustery wind of the winter night slipped inside and brought with it a gaunt-looking man in a three piece suit. He looked like he might be seven feet tall, though Marie knew that was not the case. His hair was stark white and though he looked old at first, Marie guessed he might not be any older than sixty. He had the sort of face that could look both old and young, depending on the light he was standing in.

The lanky-looking man did not speak. He simply adjusted his tie and looked around the room.

With a slight grimace and a roll of the eyes, Brendan said: "This, ladies, is Mr. Hugh Wrathe."

CHAPTER TEN

Marie found it odd that Wrathe did not bother with introductions. In fact, after finally closing the door behind him, he ventured into the sitting area. He sat down in one of the chairs and then got up three seconds later to sit in another one. He turned his large nose up to the air, sniffed, and moved to yet another one. The entire time, he did not speak to anyone.

"And you *know* that creepshow?" Marie asked.

"A bit. Conferences and events have led me to meet some very strange people. Now let's get moving before he decides to join us."

Marie noticed that Boo had only taken a few steps towards Wrathe. He sniffed in his general direction, decided he did not like what he smelled, and then huddled close to Marie. As Wrathe made his way to every chair in the sitting room, Marie, Brendan, Abagail, and Boo moved through the dining area and adjoined kitchen. Marie noticed at once that everything was new—the appliances, the light fixtures, the tile on the floor, even the countertops. Everything was also clean and glistening.

As they continued to walk around the house, Marie noticed how Abagail seemed to stick close to her. She wasn't sure if this was out of some newfound protective nature of a genuine interest in what might happen. She also noted that Brendan kept looking over to her. He was carrying some sort of thermal imaging device (she'd seen him use it in the past but could not recall the name of it) but seemed to be relying on her more than his tools.

"I don't mind the glances," she said as they made their way to the stairs, "but I don't want you to see me as just another tool. I'm not a device that takes readings."

"Sorry," he said, his face flushing a bit.

As they made their way to the stairs that led to the second floor, Marie caught sight of the patio. It sat to the back of the first floor, closed off by enormous double doors that were made of planes of glass and white framework. The curtains were pulled to the side, revealing a breathtaking view of the ocean at night. Unlike June Manor, there were no small dunes or a large stretch of back yard; the ocean was right there, no more than seventy yards or so away. She also noted that Sherry Masterson was standing there. She was doing absolutely nothing, just standing still and watching their little group make their way through the house. She was a pretty young woman but there was something about her that was creepy…not as creepy as Wrathe, but unsettling all the same.

Marie fought the urge to go out and appreciate the view. She stayed with her little group as they climbed the carpeted stairs and came to the second floor. The floors here were wood as well, with a single runner of carpet running down the center of the hall. On each side of the hallway, there were three rooms. One single room sat at the end of the hallway. It was here that they saw Katie Stillson again. She was standing in the opened doorway with her back turned, speaking to whoever was inside. Katie apparently heard them because she turned slowly around glanced at them out of the corner of her eye. She murmured something to the person in the room and then turned to face Marie and her little group.

"I want you to know," Katie said, looking directly at Marie, 'that I am not at all comfortable with you being here."

"I figured as much," Marie said. "I'm not thrilled to be here myself but if you have a legitimate need and there's something I can do to help…"

"You plan on using this as a way to earn favor with the community?"

Well, of course you'd think that, Marie thought. It was yet another comment that made her wonder if she should even be here. This went beyond too many cooks in the kitchen. With Eva Blake here, someone who didn't even seem to believe in the supernatural, and Brendan bringing his expertise, what the hell was she even doing, really?

Her snarkiness insisted that she had a place, though. And it also resulted in her rather blunt response. "Based on what I'm seeing posted in your Facebook comments threads, you may be the one that needs to worry about earning favor."

"Well, if you—"

"Ladies," Brendan said, very awkwardly stepping between them. "I can't speak for Mrs. Blake and Mr. Wrathe, but I can tell you that this sort of bickering and negative energy is going to make tonight almost impossible to carry off successfully. Please…for the sake of the investigation if nothing else, can you two try to be civil?"

The two women glared at each other for a moment. In the end, it was Katie that looked away first, her eyes going to Brendan. And when they did, Marie was pretty sure she saw them warming slightly. "Yes, I suppose I can do that," she said. "You all help yourself and make yourselves at home. If you need me for anything, just let me know."

She walked back to the stairs and no one uttered a word until she was completely out of sight.

"That woman," Abagail said quietly, "is wound a bit too tight."

Before Marie could agree, another voice spoke up. It came from the other end of the hall, from the direction of the room Katie had been standing by. "I haven't even seen or heard anything supernatural tonight and this thing is already getting tense," said a familiar female voice.

Marie turned to see Eva Clark standing in the doorway. She grinned to them and waved them over in her direction. Marie went first, followed by Brendan, Abagail, and Boo. The first thing that struck Marie about the room was that it, like everything else she'd seen, was absolutely stunning—but maybe a tad too much. It just had the feel of someone that was trying too hard. The one thing that even Marie had to admit was amazing, though, was the view. A huge picture window sat in the back wall of the room, looking out onto the ocean. The room was just high enough and the ocean at such a short distance, that only the nearest trace of the beach could be seen. From a laying-down position in the bed, it would look like the guest was floating somewhere out at sea. Marie looked away from it, not liking the stab of jealousy it brought on.

Eva had a little workstation set up at an elegant desk. Her laptop was open and there were books and papers scattered here and there. It was messy-looking but in a productive sort of way.

"I was given the master suite," she said. "But I do believe it might have originally been reserved for someone else."

"What do you mean?" Marie asked.

Eva craned her neck to look out into the hallway beyond them. When she saw the coast was clear, she said: "Well, I got the chance to speak with Katie a bit. And though I may become the enemy by saying so, she's really a charming woman. It's only when she speak about you and June Manor that she gets irritated."

“Did you happen to find out why?” Marie asked.

“Maybe a bit. I think there might be a few different reasons, one of which might be this fellow right here,” she said, nodding to Brendan. “I believe Katie’s original intent was for him to stay in this room. Based on conversations I’ve had with her, she’s quite taken with you.”

“Me?” Brendan asked. He looked genuinely confused and maybe even slightly uncomfortable.

“It’s just the vibe I picked up. She doesn’t know a ton about the supernatural community. She talks about ghosts and hauntings like a frightened kid. But somehow, she knew quite a lot about Mr. Brendan Peck.”

Marie recalled how Katie’s eyes had softened a bit after their argument once she had looked at Brendan. Was she seriously angry with her over the relationship she’d had with Brendan? If so, that seemed a little childish. Was it really worth trying to harm someone’s business over an unrequited crush?

Hey, and while we’re at it, where is this sudden urge of protectiveness over Brendan coming from? she asked herself.

“I guess that *would* explain why she was so agreeable to you coming over with me,” Brendan said. “I was expecting some push back, but there was very little. She does seem like she’s going out of her way to appease me. Even if it means bringing you along.”

“Maybe she wanted to see you together, to see how you react to one another,” Eva said, rolling her eyes. “Seems very childish to me. High school nonsense. Ah, but there are some other things, too. It’s mostly speculation and I am not one to gossip. Besides…for now, I have to remind myself that I’m here as a professional. I have a job to do and—”

“Yes, a job to do” said a voice from behind them all. Every single one of them—Marie, Eva, Abagail, Brendan, and even Boo—jumped at the shock of it. When they all wheeled around, Hugh Wrathe was standing there, peering into the room. He had come from nowhere, walking so quietly that no one had heard anything at all as he’d approached. The man moved like a phantom.

“Hi, Mr. Wrathe,” Eva said.

“We all have our jobs to do, Mrs. Blake,” he said in a monotone voice. “So could we dispense with the chatter and allow some silence for the house to rest in?”

“Yes, of course,” Eva said, lowing her eyes and gathering up a notebook and pen. Boo sniffed at Wrathe and let out a little growl.

Slowly, Marie's little group walked back down the hallway and to the stairs. "So how does this work, exactly?" Marie asked. "Are we all working together or do we go our separate ways and assume it's just like any other job?"

Brendan gave a wide, charming smile as they reached the end of the stairs. "Well, I think now is the perfect time to say something I've always looked for a reason to say in situations like these."

Wincing, Marie said, "I'm afraid to ask."

"Okay, gang! It's time to split up! Right, Scooby?"

But when Brendan looked down to Boo, it seemed as if even the dog of the group had found the joke weak and poorly timed.

CHAPTER ELEVEN

But splitting up was exactly what they did. It was decided that there might be significantly less friction for the remainder of the night if Brendan did not pair up with Marie; it would likely also make Katie a bit more agreeable. That's how the pairing ended up rather unorthodox; Marie ended up venturing around the Shoreline Oaks with Eva Blake while Abagail paired up with Brendan. Boo seemed torn over which side to take, so he settled for jaunting back and forth between the groups as the night went on.

As for the enigmatic Hugh Wrathe, he stayed on his own. And when one of the other groups accidentally happened to cross his path, he acted as if it was an enormous inconvenience. Marie did notice that Wrathe tended to stay close to where Katie was. When she was in the sitting room, drinking wine and scrolling through her phone, Wrathe sort of hovered around the kitchen. When Katie went upstairs to check on something in one of the rooms, he managed to find some reason to walk up and down the stairs. Marie also noticed that he would look disapprovingly at Eva whenever he got the chance. The looks he shot her way weren't exactly on par with the ones Katie sent towards Marie on and off throughout the night, but they were close.

Marie brought this up as she was sitting on a barstool in the area outside of the kitchen just shy of ten o' clock. "What is it with you and Wrathe?" she asked. "He keeps starring daggers at you, just in case you hadn't noticed."

"He thinks I'm trying to discredit the supernatural," Eva explained. "He believes that by trying to rationalize the paranormal with scientific means, it cheapens the mystery and magic of it all. He caused quite a scene over it at a convention a few years back."

"As far as you can tell, is he legitimate?" Marie asked.

"I think he might be. When I first heard of him, I thought he had the game rigged, you know? Like maybe he'd done vigorous research on people and used that information to exploit their loved ones. But I watched him do his thing one night when there were no cameras and no press. He was communing with the deceased brother of this woman and the way he sort of zoned out…it was odd. It creeped me right the hell out but there was something calm and peaceful about it. And the things he knew…I don't know that anyone outside of that woman would have known. Secret games they played as kids, a special hiding spot in their mom's office, favorite songs…"

"She could have told him all of that stuff beforehand," Marie pointed out.

"She could have. But the way she responded when he revealed some of this stuff…honey, I don't think there's an actress alive that could have pulled off her performance of absolute shock. She was almost scared by it. I left that scene thinking that yeah…somehow, I do think Hugh Wrathe can communicate with the other side."

"Well of course he can," said a third voice. Marie sighed deeply when she turned around, knowing it was Katie before she even saw the woman's face. Her assistant, Sherry Masterson, stood closely behind her, frowning.

"Why else do you think I asked him to come over?" Katie asked.

"The same reason you asked me," Eva commented. "But I just don't know what you expect to gain from having three differing opinions."

"Four," Marie spoke up a bit snidely.

"Because I don't understand any of this," she said. And God help her, Marie actually felt sorry for her when she saw the fear and defeat in Katie's face. "I didn't know if I should go with the scientific approach, the ghost-hunting approach, the enchanted crystal approach or what!"

"Katie," Marie said, not sure exactly how to say what she was about to put out there. "You need to know that whatever is here, there's probably some reason for it. And no…I did not put it here, despite what you may think. I just don't think we—"

She stopped here and tilted her head to the side. She hadn't heard anything but had *felt* something—or so she thought. There seemed to be a slight shift in the mood of the room. There was a sluggish sort of chill that had not been there a few moments earlier.

"What is it?" Eva asked. Katie, meanwhile, took several steps back as if she thought Marie might strike her.

"Katie, have you ever actually *seen* anything?"

"Maybe shadows here and there."

"I have," Sherry said. "Just a glimpse a few days ago, but it looked like half of a man, just from the right shoulder to his chin."

"Did you feel in danger?" Marie asked.

"No. Just scared."

"And I was pretty sure I saw a glass get pushed across the kitchen counter one time," Katie added. "But I…wait, why? What is it?"

"Do you ever feel a certain way before it happens?"

"No. But I've had a few guests say they felt cold and sort of squeezed a bit…like the air was sort of going out of the room. Why? What's going on?"

Marie stood up from the barstool and walked to the center of the room. She stood in the large foyer that sat between the sitting room and the dining area. The dreary cold feeling still clung to her. "Does anyone else feel that?"

"Feel what?" Eva asked as she, too, got to her feet.

If Marie needed further confirmation that something odd was happening, she got it just a handful of seconds later when Boo came trotting into the room. He came with a sense of urgency, looking all around. His tail was stuck straight out, rigid, as he came to Marie's side.

"What the hell is going on?" Katie asked. Beside her, Sherry trembled a bit, wide eyes looking around rapidly.

"Maybe nothing," Marie said. "There's this sort of feeling I get when I'm around paranormal activity. Sort of like a compass."

"Are you just messing with me?"

"No, I promise you that—"

She heard something go sailing through the air a moment before she saw it. She wasn't sure what it was—maybe a drinking glass or a decorative piece from the dining room, maybe—but whatever it was exploded on the floor about three feet in front of Marie. This was followed a rummaging sound behind her. She turned—along with Katie and Eva—to see every drawer in the kitchen being opened. The refrigerator shook a bit and a little to-do notepad fell to the floor.

"Oh my God…" Katie said.

Eva started scrawling in her notebook, never taking her eyes away from the commotion. Then, everything went quiet, but Marie still felt that chilling sensation. It was familiar to ones she'd felt in the past, but felt more aggressive, maybe even more prominent. She tried to get a grasp on it as she stood there, frozen. But then Boo started growling and took off towards the area behind the stairs, out towards where the patio doors sat.

Marie took off after him and that, as far as she was concerned, was how her ghost hunting venture at Shoreline Oaks began.

CHAPTER TWELVE

"Hey, Brendan, you might want to come down here!"

Marie was barely aware that Eva had even called this out up the stairs. She was too busy watching Boo. He was still growling, still on the hunt. He was walking around the secondary sitting room (because at Shoreline Oaks, that was apparently a thing) but seemed to have lost a bit of that urgency. He sniffed and let out the occasional growl, turning his nose up every now and then.

"So it's the dog that really does all of the work?" Katie asked as she watched Boo at work.

Before Marie could come up with a response, Eva said: "Dogs do have senses much more powerful than ours. You know they can sense earthquakes before they happen right?" Marie was quite happy to hear an edge of irritation in her voice.

"Well, this isn't an earthquake," Katie said. "This is a ghost. And a damned mean one at that."

Sherry Masterson, walking very closely to Katie, seemed to shiver at the words.

Marie could tell the presence was still there; it was almost like a faint itch that wouldn't go away. The issue she was having was that she was still feeling disoriented by its sudden appearance and flurry of activity. She couldn't pinpoint where it was, and it appeared that Boo was having the same problem. Yet as he continued to sniff around, he slowly made his way to the stairs. As he came to them, Brendan started coming down, followed by Abagail. They both looked excited, though Abagail also showed signs of being a little scared.

"What is it?" he asked. "I could have sworn I felt *something* coming down the stairs. A cold spot or…I don't know…"

"There was something down here," Katie said quickly.

"And it did all of that," Marie said, gesturing back to the kitchen where the drawers were still open and the shattered pieces of glass were still on the floor near where Marie had been standing. "It's the most activity I've ever seen with my eyes."

"You *saw* it?" Brendan asked.

Marie nodded, her eyes back on Boo now. He was slowly making his way up the stairs and his tail was once again taking on that odd rigid posture. His back was raised a bit, not out of anger, but caution.

"Is he onto something?" Abagail asked.

"I think so," Marie answered. She could feel everyone's eyes on her as she started up the stairs behind Boo. She felt like she was in the spotlight and for maybe the first time since discovering her gifts, she was okay with it. It was nerve-inducing, but exciting as well. Without looking back to them, she said, "Whatever it is, it's upstairs."

As if urged on by his master's voice, Boo sped up a bit and within a few seconds, Marie was once again on the second floor. She could see where Brendan had taken the time with her mother to set up some basic equipment; a few cables snaked along the floor here and there. Boo took a few steps into the hallway and then stopped. He sniffed at the floor and let out a little whine—a noise Marie rarely heard him make.

"We'll spread out," Brendan said. "Room by room, one by one. Anyone sees anything, do *not* scream. Speak quietly and make no sudden movements."

"Um, excuse me," Eva said. "But I think now might be a good time to tell everyone that I have never actually *seen* a ghost."

"But your books…" Katie said.

"Are all about the human response to the paranormal. I've spent time with more than one hundred people that have had authentic experiences with spirits, but I've never actually seen one."

"Well, maybe this will be your first," Marie said with some encouragement. It was without a doubt the strangest bit of encouragement she'd ever doled out.

"Mind if I venture into your room, Eva?"

"Help yourself," she said. Marie thought she detected an edge of fear to her voice. Was the skeptic suddenly aware that she might very well be in the middle of something genuinely scary and real?

Marie turned away, heading for the room directly in front of her. She opened the door, stepped inside, and cut on the light. When she saw the figure sitting rigidly on the edge of the bed, she nearly screamed. But by the time her throat was ready to release it, she saw the figure for what it actually was: it was only Hugh Wrathe. Sitting alone…in the dark…

"Oh, so sorry, Mr. Wrathe," Marie said. "I didn't know you—"

“The presence is not in here,” Wrathe said, without turning around to face her.

“Do you know where it is?”

“Here, there, everywhere. Wherever it wants to be.”

Marie considered asking what that meant exactly, but decided not to. She wasn’t sure she would be able to wrap her head around puzzles at the moment. Quietly, she turned the light out, slowly backed out of the room, and closed the door.

“Wow,” she said when she was back out in the hallway. She noticed Boo standing at the doorway to Eva Blake’s room so that’s where she went. The dog looked almost expectant, staring past Marie and further down the hall. He looked rather uneasy, not sure what to do. It made Marie a trifle uneasy.

She ventured into Eva’s room and saw Brendan standing in a corner with one of his handheld devices. She thought it was an EVP recorder. She quietly walked to him and saw that there was no movement on the analog bars, no digital reading of any kind. He looked to her with a disappointed frown and shrugged.

“Maybe all the commotion scared it away?” he guessed. “There was some very loud talking and sudden movements. It happens sometimes, you know.”

“Well, it all happened so fast and…”

“I know,” he said, finally looking away from the device. He looked to her and when they locked eyes the lure to kiss him was far too strong. It was almost intoxicating and it made her look away quickly.

“Marie,” he said, reaching out and taking her hand. “I really need to talk to you. I don’t know if I—”

“Brendan…I repeat: I *want* to talk about us, but not right now. I just can’t. There’s too much going on.”

“No talking now, then,” he said. “But this?”

He slowly leaned in and Marie wasted no time in even pretending she didn’t want the kiss. She leaned forward to meet him, her heart already beating hard in her chest. But before there was any contact, there was the sound of someone clearing their throat from the open bedroom door. Marie turned, already embarrassed before she saw who was standing there.

It was her mother—*of course* it was her mother. To her credit, she did her best to hide the smile that was covering the lower half of her face. “Sorry to bother you, but Eva has asked Katie for permission to go into the attic. I thought one of you might want to go with her. It seems like Boo finds the area of some interest, too."

She turned away and left them alone again. But with the moment over, things were awkward rather than romantic. "You mind going?" Brendan said. "I'd like to finish up the EVP session in here."

"Yeah," she said, her lips practically begging for her to take that kiss from him even now. She gave him a small smile and then headed back out of the room.

In the hallway, she saw that Boo *had* moved. He had walked to the first door on the left side of the hallway—the opposite side of the room Marie had found Hugh Wrathe in. He was looking curiously inside as Katie, Sherry, and Eva stepped in. Marie followed and found what, at first, looked just like another standard room.

"Mom said you guys were headed to the attic," Marie said.

"We are," Katie said, basically spitting the words out. "The entrance to the attic is here, through this room."

Inside, Marie saw a gorgeous bedroom suite, complete with a grandiose mirror hanging over a beautiful dresser. This room did not look out over the sea, but there was a fairly haunting view of the dunes along the side of the property. There were doors on both sides of the room, bumping against the far wall. She figured anyone might assume they were closets. But as Katie walked to the door on the left side and opened it up, it revealed a set of stairs. And even the stairs leading up to the attic had been given the same love and care as the rest of the house; they looked well-polished and immaculately cleaned.

"You two help yourselves," Katie said. "I'm getting back downstairs to grab a glass of wine."

"Anything we need to know about the attic?" Marie asked.

"It's cold and drafty," Katie said, already making her exit, with Sherry orbiting like a tiny moon around her. "And if I'm being totally honest, I hate going up there. It's creepy." She apparently figured this was more than enough information because with that said, she exited the room and went off to grab her glass of wine.

"After you," Eva said, clearly a little uneasy.

Marie started going up the stairs but made it no more than three stairs up before Boo came into the room. He went blasting past her, his feet clicking up the stairs as a deep growl started to issue out of his throat.

"Well, that can't be a good sign," Eva said nervously.

"Depends on how you look at it," Marie said, and started up after Boo.

CHAPTER THIRTEEN

Boo was already at the top of the stairs and making his way across the attic by the time Marie was halfway up. And it was then, as the walls started to fall away to her sides and the attic was revealed, that Marie started to feel a presence. She got the now-familiar cold chills and the sort of *pressing* feeling, as if there just wasn't quite enough room in the attic for all of them to occupy—as if the very space of the room itself was trying to squeeze them out.

"You feel that, too, right?" Eva said. "Cold…sort of cramped?"

"Yeah."

"But…if there really is some gift you have, how can I feel it?"

Marie was perplexed by how proud she was to be able to answer the question. "Everyone can feel it, I think. Spirits manifest themselves by drawing energy from the environment. A lot of times, this is felt in the presence of so-called cold spots. That's basic human sensory perception—it has nothing to do with supernatural talents."

"And whatever this is…is it up here?" Eva asked.

Marie was now at the top of the stairs, noting the way Boo was standing in the middle of the room with his tail cocked straight out. "I think it might be," Marie said. "Maybe you should go back downstairs if you don't think you can—"

"No, no, I'm fine," she said. But her tone indicated that she was far from fine.

The women entered the attic, lit by recessed lighting. It was a spacious room that currently held storage and miscellaneous items. Everything was pushed to the sides, though, and Marie could easily imagine this room somehow being converted into another master suite. It had a large window along the back wall that, like the windows in the room below, did not look out on the ocean, but got a good shot of the dunes and the coastline.

Marie felt as if they had purposefully been led up here, to the attic. There were no other room to escape to, no hiding places. For not the first time in her ghost hunting career, she felt as if *she* was the one that had been chased. And she couldn't help but feel as if she and Eva—and

Boo, of course—had been led into some sort of trap. She walked to the center of the room and stood with Boo. He backed against her, as if making sure she knew he was there for her. She nearly petted him for his loyalty but thought it might be better to keep her hands to herself when he was in this state. He had started growling again, but could not seem to choose one spot to focus on. While he remained in place, his head was constantly moving, searching for something. And all the while, Marie felt that sensation of being trapped; the air felt thicker and the room was starting to feel smaller.

"This feeling," Eva said. "Does it get any better?"

"It will eventually. Seriously, Eva…go downstairs. There's no sense in putting yourself through this."

"Nonsense. I've been writing about it for years…might as well actually experience it for myself, right? I think I'll just open this window…get some fresh air in for a bit."

"Good idea," Marie said. Suddenly, the idea of crisp winter air in the room did seem like exactly what they needed.

She paid little attention to Eva as she walked to the other end of the attic and unclasped each side of the large window—just enough to see that it was actually two windows with a seam in the center. Each side swung inside and the blast of cold air was immediate and oddly refreshing. Also odd was Boo's reaction to it. He wheeled around quickly, a snarl coming from his throat. He was looking in the opposite direction of Eva at first, over towards a stack of boxes in the corner. When Marie looked in that direction, she thought she saw something. A flicker of black, something quickly blowing outward. *Probably something laying on top of one of the boxes, blown about by the sudden gust of fresh air,* she thought.

But some other part of Marie's mind knew better. She'd seen too much to ignore something like this outright. She knew better than to—

Eva's scream broke her concentration. It was a guttural scream at first, one of pure fright and nothing more. But by the time Marie had fully turned her attention back to her, the scream had become something much more desperate and urgent…and it was easy to see why.

Eva Blake had fallen out of the window.

Marie dashed over to the window, already knowing there was nothing she'd be able to do. Unless there was some place on the roof for Eva to cling to, the only thing to stop her fall was going to be the ground. And then, just as Marie reached the open window, Eva's scream was abruptly silenced at the same time the thumping noise of her body striking the ground floating up on the icy air.

Marie did not waste any time looking down out of the window. Instead, she ran out of the attic. She forgot about the potential spirit and even the entire reason for being at Shoreline Oaks in the first place. She exited the attic so fast that she nearly fell down the stairs. When she exited the bedroom, she nearly collided with her mother in the hallway.

"Marie, what is it?" Abagail asked.

"Eva…she fell out of the attic window," Marie called as she raced to the stairs leading downstairs. Her heart was thumping and tears were forming in her eyes.

"She *what?"*

But Marie did not bother to stop and give an answer. She ran through the sitting area and the large foyer and for a moment, it seemed as it was taking far too long. It almost felt like the house was doing everything it could to keep her from getting outside. She knew it was a crazy thought, but it was there nonetheless. When she finally did make it through the house and out of the front door, the winter night didn't feel quite as cold as it had felt up in the attic as it had come through the windows.

Marie leaped down the stairs with agility she wasn't aware she still had and ran around the edge of the yard where the large attic window had been facing out. There, she saw Eva Blake's body on the ground. Right away, any hope of the woman simply sustaining a broken leg or a few busted ribs was dashed. She could tell right away from the posture of the body and the unblinking eyes looking directly at her that Eva Blake was dead.

As her mind processed all of this, she also saw the three people standing around the body. One of them was Sherry Masterson, standing by Katie Stillson. A glass of wine was in Katie's right hand, trembling, while her other hand covered her mouth in shock. Beside her, Hugh Wrathe looked down to the body as if he might be inspecting a strange flower growing in the yard.

Katie turned around and glowered at her. "What happened?" she asked. Then, as if the thought was just occurring to her, she freed her left hand from her mouth and used it to point an accusing finger at Marie. *"What did you do?"*

Marie ignored her completely, unable to take her eyes off of Eva's body. She felt numb, almost as if her soul was floating just outside of her body, trying to escape the absolute absurdness of the situation. Behind her, she could hear several sets of footsteps coming down the porch stairs and hurrying across the yard.

"Marie?" Brendan said, a tremor in his voice. When she turned to him, she saw something almost like relief in his face. *He thought it was me,* she thought. *He thought I was the one that fell out the window...*

In front of her, Wrathe carefully knelt by Eva's body. He checked her pulse with a strange sort of calm and care. He waited a moment and then looked around at everyone, speaking out loud what Marie had already assumed.

"Dead," he said simply.

Marie, who by this point during her time in Port Bliss, was all too familiar with being around the recently deceased, pulled out her phone with arms that were trembling almost violently.

"Everyone step away," she said. And even before she pulled up the number to the police department, she was already imagining how Sherriff Miles was going to react.

CHAPTER FOURTEEN

Marie watched the headlights of Sheriff Miles's police car come bouncing along the front windows of Shoreline Oaks just after midnight. Katie Stillson made a point to be the one standing at the door when the car parked and two figures got out of the car. Marie had tried on one occasion to take that position, wanting to speaking to Miles before anyone else, but Katie held her ground firmly. And honestly, Marie didn't see the point in causing any unnecessary drama on a night that was already filled with it.

So she sat in one of the armchairs in the sitting room and watched as Katie opened the door for Sheriff Miles and Officer Creighton. Marie saw that Creighton was looking off to the side of the porch as she entered, looking over to where Eva Blake had fallen. Miles took a look around the room and looked baffled. It appeared as if he wanted to start talking several times but then stopped, thought of a better way to start, and then finally got a word out.

"I've got forensics from the State PD on the way, and the local medical examiner about thirty seconds behind me," he said. "Before we can be interrupted by any of them, I need to know what happened. If you weren't in the room with the deceased or if you did not see her come out of the window, don't bother talking right now. You can speak with me later but for right now, there will be *no* cross-talking. Mrs. Stillson, this is your home, so you can begin."

Katie nodded vigorously, more than happy to tell what she knew. "I was standing right there by the kitchen sink," she said, pointing to the left, "and saw something *fall.* But I heard the scream first. I heard the scream and then saw her and…it was Marie Fortune! She did it, she's the one who—"

"And Ms. Fortune, what about you?" Miles asked, interrupting. "Were you with her when it happened?"

"Yes," Marie said, feeling the weight of that one syllable. "I was upstairs with her. We were in the attic, and she said she wanted to open the windows because it was thick up there."

"Thick?" Miles asked.

"Stuffy. Just sort of cramped and hot. She wanted fresh air. So she opened the windows. Next thing I knew, she was screaming and she had fallen out of the window."

"You didn't see it happen?" Miles asked.

"No."

He thought about this for a moment as another car pulled up into the driveway. Creighton whispered something into is ear and then walked outside to meet the new arrivals—presumably the medical examiner.

When Creighton was outside, Miles looked around the room and nodded curtly to Brendan. "Good to see you again, Mr. Peck."

"Likewise."

"If you're here and Marie is here, can I assume there's something ghost-related going on?"

"We believe so, yes," Brendan said.

"It's true, Sherriff," Katie said. "There's something bad here…and I don't want to admit that it's a ghost, but I don't see any other way to explain it."

"And who was this other woman?" Miles asked. "The woman that fell out of the window?"

"Eva Blake," Marie said. "She was a psychologist studying the effects of the paranormal of the human mind."

Another voice spoken up, seemingly out of nowhere. Everyone jumped, startled, even Miles. Apparently, Hugh Wrathe had managed to somehow show up in his almost ghostly way.

"She was incorrect in a lot of her theories," he said, "but she always had the best of intentions."

"I see," Miles said. "And who are you, sir?"

"Hugh Wrathe. Psychic. Paranormal enthusiast."

"And did you see or hear anything?"

"Only the screaming, Before that, I was in the ether where only the voices and ways of the dead exist."

"Oh, okay…so…and what about you?" Miles asked, quickly moving away from the crazy answer and looking to Abagail.

"I'm Abagail Fortune…Marie's mother."

"Oh. Well, it's nice to meet you. I know your daughter fairly well, you know." He then leveled a glance at Marie that held a little too much weight to it for Marie's taste and added: "Maybe a little too well."

“As for now, I’d like all of you to stay put. Except you, Mrs. Stillson. Would you mind showing me to the room where Mrs. Blake fell from the window?”

“Of course,” Katie said. When she made her way across the room and towards the stairs, she made a point to give Marie a wide berth.

With Katie gone, Marie finally got out of her chair and walked over to the kitchen. She looked out of the window and though she could not see the exact spot where Eva had landed, she could see a few people moving around. She saw Creighton’s tall figure, as well as two men. One of them was taking pictures, the other setting up a little mobile searchlight.

She was vaguely aware of Brendan approaching from behind. “You and Miles are going to keep being entwined until your dying day, it seems,” he said.

“It’s starting to feel that way.”

“Well at least this will be one situation where you clearly can’t be considered a suspect. I mean…she fell from the window, right?”

She started to nod, but then stopped. She recalled the moments before Eva’s fall. She’s screamed two different times. The second scream had clearly been the shrieking sort of desperation in knowing death waited a few stories below. But that first one—that had been a scream of pure fright. Had she seen something or felt something in the seconds leading up to going out of the window? Had something attacked her?

“What is it?” Brendan asked.

“I think whatever it is that’s haunting this place might have…I don’t know…maybe it could have had something to do with it?”

“I don’t know, Marie. Even I’ve only heard a handful of stories about poltergeists actually being responsible for someone’s death. And in almost every single instance, it has turned out to be false.”

“But you do understand how *weak* that explanation sounds, right?” Marie asked. “That she *fell?* During a paranormal investigation involving me, a woman that has somehow managed to stumble into far too many murder investigations…she just *fell.”*

As if summoned by the theory itself, Officer Creighton came walking into the house. She bristled a bit as she came from the cold, into the warm house. She looked around for a while and then said: “Where’s Sheriff Miles?”

“Upstairs with Katie,” Marie said.

Creighton gave her a quick nod, and Marie did *not* like the look that came across her face. She said nothing about it, though, and started back for the chair she'd been sitting in. Before she got to it, though, the sound of footsteps started coming down the stairs. Miles and Katie were coming back down the stairs. Katie had a slightly shaken expression on her face, while Miles's own expression was rather grim. It grew even tighter when he saw Creighton waiting for him.

"Sheriff, a word, please," Creighton said.

They walked over to the secondary sitting room while Katie rejoined the others in the larger sitting area.

"Forgive me for asking," Wrathe said, his voice slow and monotone. "But given the events that have transpired, I believe I would like to leave. I see no point in furthering this session."

"Yes, I understand that," Katie said. "But Sheriff Miles has asked that everyone stay here for a while. No one is to leave. I can, of course, offer you a complimentary room for your troubles."

"Much obliged," Wrathe said, though he actually looked a little disappointed. "Just, not the one that connects to the attic, please."

The conversation between Miles and Creighton did not last very long. Less than a minute later, they both came back into the larger sitting room. Creighton eventually headed back out with the ME and his partner while Miles sighed deeply and took yet another long glance around the room.

"I need everyone to stay put," he said. "Mrs. Stillson has assured me that she has plenty of room for everyone. Given the nature of what happened and the size of this house, we'll need to speak to each of you individually." He paused here and then set his eyes solely on Marie. "Ms. Fortune—Marie—would you please come with me?"

His constant use of *Ms. Fortune* had her on edge. The look of regret and irritation in his eyes did not help, either.

"What is it?" she asked. "Is everything okay?"

"I'd just like to talk to you elsewhere…away from all of this."

"Well, can I just—"

"No. I'll ask just once more but if you don't come along easily, I'll have to make it handcuff official."

"Handcuffs?" Marie gasped.

"Yeah, sorry," Abagail said. "That's crap."

Marie was surprised and, oddly, a little moved by the anger in her mother's voice. It was the second time in the past few days that her mother had stood up for her. But sensing that the entire situation was really nothing more than a time bomb ticking away, Marie shook her head. “It’s okay, Mom. Sure, Sheriff. Let’s go.”

“But, Marie,” Abagail said.

“She’ll be fine,” Brendan said. He then looked to Miles and Creighton with something like contempt. “We’ll see her soon enough. Trust me.”

Miles and Creighton made no response. Instead, Miles gave Marie the slightest little nudge towards the front door. When they were out on the porch, she could still hear her mother objecting from inside. As Miles led her down the porch stairs, she looked to the right, to where the ME and his partner were still taking pictures. She noted that one of them had placed an extended tape measure between the place where Eva had fallen and the edge of the house.

“I’m coming along willingly,” Marie pointed out, “but I never heard you actually state that I was under arrest.”

“That was for myself as well as you,” Miles said as they reached the patrol car. “I did not want to give Katie Stillson the satisfaction. Also, there’s not quite enough evidence just yet. But this way is best for everyone.”

“This way? You mean placing me in the back of a police car? I mean, what the hell is it you think I’ve done?”

“I’m not going to make any proclamations just yet,” Miles said. “But even my rather untrained eye can agree with the findings the examiner was able to determine pretty quickly.”

“And what findings were those?” Marie asked, her voice now shaking as Miles opened the back driver’s side door of his patrol car.

“The distance is just too great,” Miles said as Marie slid into the back of the car. “It seems pretty clear that Eva Blake did not simply fall. She was pushed. And by your own admission, you were the only person in the room with her when it happened.”

That said, Miles closed the door and Marie found herself looking back to the Shoreline Oaks. She saw figures looking out from the door but as the car was cranked, they may as well have been looking out to her from some other, distant world. Marie wasn’t sure she’d ever felt so alone, so helpless…or so afraid.

CHAPTER FIFTEEN

"You know, I was always afraid you'd end up in one of these," Miles said from the other side of the table. They were sitting in one of the Port Bliss PD's two interrogation rooms and Miles looked almost as uncomfortable as Marie felt. He was holding a cup of coffee but not drinking from it and Marie could not help but get a sort of disappointed father vibe from him; he was the dad and she was the seventeen-year-old that had come in an hour late after curfew.

"I think deep down, maybe I did, too," Marie said. "But, of course, you know I didn't push that woman."

"That's the thing, Marie. I feels sort of like that troll under the bridge, letting all the goats walk on across, one right after the other. And I fear if I keep doing it, I'm eventually going to get a big set of horns right up my backside."

It hurt a bit, but she also did her best to understand where he was coming from. In less than a year—hell, in less than nine months, this was the sixth time she'd come face to face with Miles because she was a suspect in a murder case. She supposed she might even think he was bad at his job if he didn't at least throw *some* suspicion her way.

"So what can I do?" she asked. "What do you need to know?"

"I need to know what happened in that room," he said. "You were the only ones up there. And if I'm being honest, the whole inclusion of the ghost hunting thing is not making me any more comfortable with how it all went down."

"It was just like I told you back at the house," she said. As she started to defend herself, she became much more aware that she was actually in an interrogation room. This was a brand new level of trouble.

"Well, let's go back a bit further. When did you first meet Eva Blake?"

"Earlier today. She came by June Manor, on her way to Shoreline Oaks. She wanted to speak with me because she'd heard about me in some of those online articles."

"And what was Mrs. Blake's business there with Mrs. Stillson, from your point of view?"

"Katie believes there is a particularly nasty ghost in her house—an entity known as a poltergeist. I should also point out, I suppose, that she somehow thinks I put it there. But I guess that's beside the point. Eva Blake is an author. She writes about how the paranormal and supernatural are likely all just manifestations of certain mindsets—that there are really no such thigs as ghosts or the afterlife. Because Katie called Eva *and* Brendan, I'm assuming she was just looking to have a level playing field. She wanted opinions from both sides."

"I can't believe I'm about to ask you this, but…do you believe there's a ghost there?"

"Yes. Based on what I saw and what I experienced tonight, I believe that beyond a shadow of a doubt."

"And you believe it pushed Eva Blake out of a window."

Marie was careful here, not wanting to project a crazy theory as truth. "I don't know," she said. "All I know is I heard her cry out and when I turned, she was falling out of the window. I suppose there was a good chance she fell out but to me, that just doesn't seem likely."

"And there were no cameras in the room?" Miles asked. "No evidence to support that you did not push her?"

The answer flared in her head like a fire and she knew the weight it would carry. It made it that much harder to answer. "No."

"Did you and Mrs. Blake have any interactions throughout the night other than when you were up in that room?"

"Yes, plenty."

"And everyone else saw these interactions?"

"Yes."

Miles sighed and got to his feet, still holding his coffee. "Well, I hate to do it to you, but I do need you to stay here, in this room for a bit. Before I came in, your mother and that Peck fellow came in through the front doors, insisting to speak to me. I'm going to get their stories and then ride out to speak to Mrs. Stillson and that other fellow…what was his name?"

"Hugh Wrathe. Another paranormal guy. Sort of a psychic."

"Of course he is," Miles said, gently massaging the bridge of his noise, as if pushing a headache away. "Just…hold tight, okay?"

Marie nodded, not liking the idea of being holed up in this room by herself at all. Oddly enough, as she watched Miles leave, she started to feel scared—not of the situation itself, but of being alone in this small room. Apparently, she was okay chasing after mean-spirited ghosts but when it came to being alone in a featureless room with only her thoughts, she started to lose her nerve. And she wondered what, exactly, that said about her.

She remained there for about half an hour, staring at the walls and trying to recall exactly how she'd come to be here. Moving to Port Bliss had been the scariest thing she'd ever done but it had netted the largest reward possible. She had friends, a mostly successful business that she'd always dreamed of, and had somehow even reunited with her mother. Yet here she was now, in an interrogation room, having just been questioned by a sheriff she had come to respect a great deal. Life really could be polarizing and unexpected at times, that was for sure.

When Miles came back in, she could see the uncertainty on his face. He sat back down across from her like there was an immense weight on his shoulders.

"Your mother and Brendan are adamantly insisting there's no way you killed Eva Blake. This is not surprising, of course. But Brendan claims the footsteps he heard from upstairs basically proves your innocence. He says he heard two initial cries of distress from Mrs. Blake. The first one was sort of a surprised yelp. The second…well, that was when she was falling. There were a series of really fast, sort of thunderous footsteps between them. That's his story, anyway but he also admits that from downstairs, there could have been a lot he missed out on."

"So in other words, no *strong* evidence exists?"

"It doesn't seem that way," Mile said. "From where I stand, and based on everything I know, I don't have any reason to think you would kill that woman. But based on the evidence at hand, it's something I have to consider." He sighed and looked Marie in the eyes with a great deal of sympathy. "Is there anything else? If not, I should probably join Officer Creighton back out at the house. If there's anything that can prove you did *not* push Eva Blake, we'll find it."

"No," she said, slightly defeated. "There's nothing else."

"Absolutely right," he said. "Now, the faster I can get back out there and help, the sooner I can get you out of this interrogation room."

Marie nodded and Miles instantly got up and started for the door. Just before he opened it, Marie called out. She simply couldn't help it. She had to say *something*—just one more thing before he left."

“Sheriff…you know me. You know I didn’t do this.”

He almost opened his mouth to say something. She was pretty sure it was going to be *“I know.”* But in the end he gave her that same sympathetic look and simply nodded. He then left Marie alone in the room, her future in his hands.

CHAPTER SIXTEEN

Sheriff Miles was true to his word. He did his best to not make Marie wait too long in the interrogation room. When he stepped back in, it was just two hours after he'd left her the first time; Marie's watched read 2:10 a.m. They were both clearly tired when he came back in the room. He did not sit down across from her, maybe because he feared he might fall asleep.

"You're too tired for me to read your face," Marie said. "I don't know if you come bearing good news or bad."

"It's very neutral…as always."

"Okay…"

"The good news is that I'm letting you go. For now. Katie Stillson is adamant that you had something to do with Mrs. Blake falling, but she has no proof. The other guy, Hugh Wrathe, seems to be off on some other planet, but he also thinks the idea of you pushing Mrs. Blake out of that window is ridiculous. The other employee that was on hand—Sherry Masterson—says she only heard the screaming and that was all. She claims to not have seen or heard enough to make any sort of snap judgment…something her employer could maybe take a lesson from, if we're being honest."

Marie found it almost sweet that the odd nature of Hugh Wrathe would allow him to so quickly support her innocence. But Katie…well, that was a whole different story, wasn't it?

"So where does that leave us?" Marie asked.

"It leaves me with no evidence either way. Even if you *did* push her, I'm being told by forensics that there would likely not be a good enough hand or fingerprint on Mrs. Blake's shirt to pull from. Speaking of prints, there's nothing worthwhile up in that attic—just prints from you and Mrs. Blake. No footprints of any kind to show if you did indeed walk over to push her. So, right now we have only two speculations: that she fell, or you pushed her."

"There *is* a third," Marie pointed out.

"Maybe, but I am not about to type down in my report that there's an option that Mrs. Blake was pushed out of the window by a ghost."

He shook his head in disbelief and said, “One thing is for certain, Marie. You sure have made my life a lot more interesting.”

“Is that a good thing or a bad thing?”

“Both, But right now…bad. Look, get home. Get some rest. But also know that we’ll likely come to question you, your mother, and Brendan again. How long are they in town?”

Marie got to her feet and shrugged. “Your guess is as good mine.”

“Let them know I need them to stick around for at least another forty-eight hours.”

Marie headed for the door, which Miles opened. She paused for a moment, feeling that disappointed father sensation from him again. “You know,” she said, “I really am very sorry we keep having these…these *situations.”*

“You and me both,” Miles said as he closed the door and escorted Marie down the hall where the release paperwork was waiting for her.

***

Marie was not at all surprised to find her mother and Brendan in the sitting room, waiting for her. There was a small part of her that had half expected Posey and Rebeka to be waiting, too. But Posey was at home tonight, and Rebeka was apparently upstairs, asleep—exactly where these two should also be. Boo was also there, and when she opened the door he instantly came rushing to her side.

“It’s 3:45 in the morning,” Marie told them as she came into the room. “Go to sleep.”

“What’s the verdict?” Abagail asked with all the enthusiasm of a practiced lawyer.

“There wasn’t enough evidence to convict me straight away, so I’m technically free for now. But the investigation is ongoing. It would be really nice if neither of you left in the next two days.”

“I’m not going anywhere,” Abagail said.

“Same here,” Brendan said. She appreciated the soft, caring look he sent her way. But it also made her want to go to him, lose herself in his arms and just bawl this whole thing out.

“Surely with everyone that was there, something will have to prove your innocence, right?” Abagail asked.

“I don’t know,” Marie said. “But I’m a little too familiar with these sorts of things. And I know it’s almost never as easy as it seems. We can talk about it tomorrow, but for right now…I just need to go to sleep."

"Marie…" Abagail said.

"It's okay, Mom." Just saying that word—*mom*—seemed surreal. "Goodnight to both of you." She looked to Brendan last, trying to return that soft and caring glance he'd given her moments ago, but she was pretty sure hers just looked very sleepy.

She made her way to her room with Boo falling in behind her. Before she could close the door and start to change for bed, she heard her name whispered. For a desperate moment, she was sad that it wasn't Brendan.

"Marie?" her mother said. "I know you're tired, but I did want to share one thing with you. Maybe it's something you've already pieced together on your own, but it needs to be said."

"What is it?" Marie asked, opening the bedroom door so her mother could enter.

"Brendan filled me in on some of the other times you've gotten wrapped up in murder cases. I hope you know it's not you…and I suppose it might not even be the gift."

"I'm not following you, Mom. I'm very tired and I—"

"People can sort of *sense* the gift on you. It's almost like we cast some sort of spell on them. People will come to you for help on things they might not otherwise have. People may trust you a bit more. I've seen it myself, too. Of course, none of my experiences ever got me knotted up with the police. I suppose the Sheriff sensed it on you. I mean…how else were you never properly arrested for any of your little adventures?"

"I guess that does make a bit of sense. But still…"

"During my travels in looking for answers, it has helped me to get to know people. I've made some wonderful friends because they had come to me for help—people I hardly knew at all, just sort of getting this feeling about me. But then the truth would come out—usually because I told them—and those people would grow distant. Things got awkward."

Marie thought of her relationship with Robbie and how it had soured a bit when she'd come forward with the truth. She thought of the rather odd relationship she had with Sheriff Miles…and her mother's explanation absolutely checked out.

"Do you resent the gift?" Abagail asked, seemingly out of the blue.

Marie almost answered *yes* right away, but then hesitated. She thought of seeing Aunt June. She even thought of some of the scarier moments of the past several months and how, even when there was the fear there, she'd also felt a childlike awe and wonder—the inkling of an idea that she was *so close* to what waited for everyone once this life was done.

"I don't know," she answered. "I'm too tired to process it all."

"Okay. Get some rest, sweetie."

With that, Abagail left the room, closing the door behind her. Marie got changed for bed, brushed her teeth, and collapsed into bed. Sleep came quickly, but she did not sleep well.Dark dreams were waiting for her, like a monster in the darkness.

She saw herself standing on the back patio of June Manor. Her mother was standing out on the beach with a suitcase in her hand. She was speaking with Aunt June, and neither of them knew she was looking. It looked like her mother was crying, and June was consoling her. Then, after the two lightly embraced, Abagail started walking out into the water. The waves crashed all around her but seemed to carve themselves open to allow her to pass. When she was out in the water up to her chest, Marie called out. Her mother did not turn around, but Aunt June did; she smiled and waved at Marie, not caring about Abagail right behind her.

As Abagail's head went underwater, Marie took off down the patio stairs. There, she found Brendan, playing with Boo in the back yard. When Boo saw her, he growled at her. His back arched upwards and he took a defensive stance.

"Boo? It's okay, it's m—"

Boo unleashed a series of snarls and barks while Brendan petted him. He smiled up at her and laughed. "You didn't think we'd stay forever, did you?"

"I don't understand," she said. "I chose you."

"Did you *really*, though?"

She opened her mouth to say something but it was drowned out by the roaring crash of a wave that struck the ground right at the edge of the back yard. Seawater came rushing towards the house, flooding the yard. She looked out towards the beach and found the shore gone, water from the ocean. Another wave crashed, and this time it carried Marie away with it as it coasted forward, smashing into the house, breaking windows and soaking everything inside of June Manor.

Boo came swimming by and when he saw her, he opened his jaws and bit down hard on her arm and—

Marie came awake, her heart slamming in her chest. Boo was nuzzling at her, whining. Apparently, she'd been thrashing in her sleep and he'd come up onto the bed to check on her.

"That's a good boy," Marie said, patting the bed next to her.

He lay down, tail wagging lazily, and let her snuggle into him. She listened to his light breathing and though it was comforting, it took her a long time to fall back to sleep. And when she did, she could swear she tasted a faint trace of seawater in the back of her throat.

More than that, though, the dream left her feeling displaced…as if June Manor may not be as permanent as she thought.

CHAPTER SEVENTEEN

The first thing Marie saw when she left her bedroom the following morning shortly after eight o'clock was Posey's face. She was in the dining room, eating scrambled eggs and toast. Marie knew that when Posey ate something so simple and rustic, there was something weighing heavy on her mind. It was one of the very rare instances where Marie was glad there weren't any guests currently residing in June Manor.

"Marie," Posey said, giving her a forlorn look. "I just heard about everything that happened last night. I'm so sorry. You poor thing. You must feel like you're cursed or something."

"Sometimes that's not too far from the truth." She let out a yawn and walked over to the coffee pot. "Who told you? Or did you get it all from social media and Nosy Nellies blowing up your phone?"

"Some phone calls, some texts," Posey admitted. "But I got most of it out of from one of your guests. Good looking fellow that just can't seem to stay out of your life."

Marie doctored her coffee and joined Posey at the table. "Posey, it looks like it might be really bad this time. I don't think…wait. Hold one. Have you seen Brendan or my mother this morning?"

"Brendan, yes. He left about half an hour ago to take Boo for a walk. As for your mother, she's still asleep as far as I know."

At the mention of Brendan taking Boo for a walk, images of last night's dream popped into her head. She swallowed down some coffee in the hopes of chasing it away.

"Okay…so what's the buzz online? What sort of a monster am I?"

"Well, believe it or not, there are more people thinking it's more likely a ghost had something to do with Eva's death than you did."

"I guess that's…a good thing?"

"I'd say so.," Posey said. "There are some very interesting conversations taking place and people are admitting they not only believe in ghosts, but sharing some of their experiences and sightings. I think I've told you…this part of the state has always been entrenched in ghost stories. So now it's not only arguments about whether or not you had anything to do with it, but people arguing back and forth about the legitimacy of ghost sightings."

"Oh yes, I'm well aware. But I guess it's a good thing that people are having those sorts of conversations."

"Now, I won't lie," Posey went on. "The people that aren't especially on your side are being quite mean about things. Some are saying this should be what finally exposes you and runs you out of town. There was one comment that even suggested you might be a witch."

"Ah, I was wondering how long that might take," Marie said. But it was only in an attempt to shield herself from the sting and hurt of it. "So I take it most of the town now knows what happened out there at Shoreline Oaks?"

"They know that Eva Blake died from falling out of a window and that she was either pushed or fell out. And they know your name is wrapped up in it all." She sat her phone down (screen-side against the table, Marie noticed) and looked earnestly to Marie. "And what does our esteemed Sheriff Miles think happened?"

"He's a bit more uncertain that usual," Marie said. "Not that I blame him."

"Do you plan on doing what you usually do?"

"And what do I usually do?" Marie asked with just a bit of edge to her voice.

"Do all the police work. Become a detective. Figure the whole thing out for yourself and clear your name."

Marie shook her head slowly. It was funny, though; there had been a few times in the recent past that she had actually considered whether or not she had the chops to make it as a detective. "Not this time," she said. "Even if I wanted to, it's not like I can just roll up in Katie Stillson's house and ask to look around." She chuckled and shook her head. "Lord only knows the sort of venom she's spewing on Facebook this morning."

"Actually, Katie has been oddly silent on the whole thing," Posey said. "I haven't seen a single thing out of her."

"Maybe she's still asleep," Marie said. "I think it was a long night for everyone involved." But deep down, she wondered if there might be some other reason. She had seen what Katie had been dealing with last night. Linking a murder up to that sort of activity was liable to torment anyone. God help her, but Marie almost felt sorry for the woman.

When the front door opened, Marie almost expected Miles to come walking in, handcuffs at the ready, telling her there was a cell at the state prison with her name on it. But then she recalled that Miles always knocked when he paid a visit. Moments later, Brendan and Boo made their way into the room. Boo hurried over to Marie, resting his head on her leg as if to make sure she was doing better than she had been last night.

"Damn, it's cold out there," Brendan said.

"All that sun out west has made you soft," Posey said.

"How are you?" Brendan asked, looking to Marie. His cheeks were red from the chill outside. It made him look young and somehow mischievous.

"I don't know. What's the word on the street?"

"I didn't really get any information," he said. "I'm assuming there are some people in town that know who I am and are doing their best to stay away."

"Welcome back to Port Bliss," Marie said with an unsteady smile. "The welcome wagon appears to be broken."

"Don't blame it all in the town," another voice said from the entrance between the sitting room and the dining room. Abagail stood there, still looking rather tired. "It's the people that have it all messed up."

"Good morning," Marie said. "Sleep well?"

"No. I was too worried about you. I don't mean to come into town guns all a-blazing, but isn't there something we can do to figure this out? Something we can maybe do to solve this on our own?"

At once, Posey and Brendan looked to Marie with a smile. Marie said nothing, though her own smiled started to form.

"What?" Abagail asked.

"You sound just like your daughter," Posey said.

"She's been making a habit of getting into trouble and then figuring a way out of it on her own for the last several months," Brendan said.

"Ah, a stubborn and determined streak," Abagail said as she made her way over to the coffee pot. "It's good to know you got *something* from me other than this so-called gift."

"So-called?" Marie asked.

"Yeah. I mean, it doesn't seem too much like a gift right now, does it?"

"No, I guess not," Marie said. "But like all the times before, I think I might be able to use it to get me out of this mess. That is…if I can get a little help."

"I thought you said you wouldn't be doing the detective-thing," Posey said.

"This isn't really being a detective," Marie said. "This is more like…just *snooping.*"

"Ooh," Abagail said, pouring her coffee. "What do you need?"

She sat down to the table, as did Brendan and Posey, as Marie rolled through what was not quite a plan, but had the underpinnings of one. It started, as most plans do, by going over the available information—which, in this case, was not much.

"Let's face it," she said. "It's pretty clear why I'm the primary suspect. I was the only one up there with her. Even Boo wasn't in the room, though he was lurking around somewhere up there with us. But I was also the one closest to the door, to the stairs. If anyone had snuck in to push Eva, I would have seen them. It's not like someone came in while I wasn't paying attention, did it, and then left. Not only would that be impossible, but I would have seen them."

"And Eva didn't seem like the sort of have any enemies," Abagail said. "You liked her for the most part, right?"

"She was a little snotty about her beliefs and had this unspoken way of looking down on paranormal believers, but other than that, yeah."

"You just nailed the *exact* way most people at conventions feel about her, too," Brendan commented.

"I liked her well enough, Katie seemed to like her and Wrathe…well, who knows what he was thinking."

"So let's look at the list of people that were in the house at the time she fell," Brendan said. "There was the three of us, Eva herself, Wrathe, Katie, and that one employee…what was her name?"

"Sherry Masterson," Abagail answered.

"And I think I'm okay to eliminate the three of us," Marie said. She then looked to her mother giving her a look that was meant to be funny. "Right?"

"What?" Abagail said, incredulous. "No, I did not kill that woman! You just said yourself that—"

"Just messing with you," Marie said, doing what she could to dredge up some humor to inject into the situation.

“Here’s the other thing to note,” Brendan said, side-stepping Marie’s attempt at a joke. “If we take us out of the equation, the other three people were all downstairs when Eva fell. So even if someone *could* sneak in and out of there, it becomes a non-issue.”

“So…it was the poltergeist,” Abagail said.

“Seems that way,” Marie said.

“I looked over my footage from last night,” Brendan said. “Granted, there was very little and I was nowhere near the attic when it happened, so I can offer nothing there.”

“I need to go back,” Marie said, already stitching a plan together in her head. She knew where she needed to go, but she had split feelings over it. “Somehow, I need to get back into that attic. But it’s not like Katie is going to welcome me back to her place with open arms.”

“What good would that do?” Posey asked. She had not spoken yet and had more or less been a bystander.

“That poltergeist did not mind showing itself when I was around the first time,” Marie said. “I wonder if I might be able to provoke it…get it to show itself again.”

“I don’t know about that,” Brendan said. “That sounds incredibly dangerous.”

“I’ll be safe, I think,” she said. “I’ll take Mom with me.”

“You will?” Abagail asked. She looked both privileged and terrified at the same time.

Ignoring her, Marie then looked to Brendan. “And you will be the one to get her out of the house for us.”

“How so?”

“Well, according to Eva, she clearly has a thing for you. Why don’t you invite her out for lunch? Maybe let her know how sorry you are that this all happened.”

Posey chuckled at this as she got up from the table. “I should maybe walk away,” she said. “Don’t want to be aiding and abetting a break-in attempt.”

“Wait, is that what you’re proposing?” Abagail asked. “Breaking into this woman’s place of business?”

Marie understood how it sounded and for a moment, even considered that it might be going too far. But she also knew she had to act quickly, that there was no time for hesitation.

"Maybe," she said, a bit nervous. "It's not like I'll be stealing anything. I'm going in there to try to figure out how and why a woman was killed—and to potentially clear my name."

Brendan and Abagail shared a look. Boo trotted around under the table, waiting for someone to start eating breakfast so he could gather up the crumbs. Brendan petted the dog idly and said, "So when did you want to start?"

Marie thought of the concern she'd seen in Miles last night, and heard the shrieking of Eva Blake as she fell to her death. She gave a deep sigh and said: "No time like the present."

Brendan nodded and slowly dug out his phone. He looked at it for a moment and said, "Are you sure about this?"

"No. But I think it's the best bet."

"Okay," Brendan said. "Time to turn on the charm."

He called Katie Stillson right there in front of them, officially kicking off what Marie was already starting to feel was a shaky plan at best.

CHAPTER EIGHTEEN

"I should probably point out that I'm not a very good liar," Abagail said as she pulled her car into the Shoreline Oaks driveway.

"I don't need you to lie," Marie said. "I just need you to make sure Sherry isn't looking out of windows or doorways. I need you to keep her downstairs. Tell her you're very upset that Katie is being so accusatory. See if she'll give you *her* side of what she experienced when Eva fell."

"I'm still nervous about it."

"Oh, I am, too," Marie said. "Believe it or not, your daughter isn't a fan of sneaking around into other people's houses."

"I always thought if we ever reunited, it would be this really touching sunset scene, or maybe a fancy dinner," Abagail said. "But I never would have imagined this."

"Yeah, sorry about that."

Marie thought that out of the three of them, Brendan was likely having the best time—being fawned over and getting to enjoy lunch. Meanwhile, she felt her stomach gurgling and bubbling with nerves as her mother parked the car. Much like June Manor, it appeared that Shoreline Oaks was lacking guests on the week between Christmas and New Year's Eve; there was only one other vehicle in the gravel parking lot.

"I'll give you one minute before I get out," Marie said. "I hope you're good at thinking on the fly."

"I am. I'm also quite good at going on and on with a conversation even when it's clear the other person wants it to be over."

"Perfect," Marie said, slinking further down in the seat. "And I need you to try to get her on the back patio. Maybe act all impressed with the view."

"You think that'll really work?"

"Not sure. But there's only one way to find out, right?"

Abagail let out a shaky sigh, opened her door, and exited the car. For a moment, Marie could hear her footfalls on the gravel, then on the sidewalk, and then not at all. A few seconds later, there was the very distant sound of someone knocking on the door and then, a handful of moments after that, the sound of two people murmuring. The sound of the door closing came not too long after that. Marie looked to her watch, waited a very tense minute, and then quietly got out of the car.

She hurried across the lawn and walked up to the porch as if she was afraid she might step on a landmine. When she came to the door, she reached out for the handle and looked behind her. She was certain Katie would pull up behind her at any moment. But she knew this was not the case, as Katie was scheduled to meet with Brendan for lunch five minutes ago. Marie placed her ear to the door and heard her mother's voice. It was getting further and further away. She then heard someone laughing—not her mother, but someone else. Sherry, presumably. After another few moments, their voices were still present and Marie didn't think her mother would succeed in moving Sherry outside.

Got to take that chance, Marie thought. She started to turn the doorknob and then heard another door closing inside. Hopefully it her mother and Sherry heading out onto the patio.

Marie turned the knob and opened the door. When she realized she could see her mother and Sherry through the large open glass panes along the back of the house, she skirted quickly to the left. She essentially hugged the kitchen wall as she made her way to the stairs. As she started ascending them, she could hear Sherry's voice from outside. She sounded a little stern, but not overly confrontational.

The next problem in the plan, of course, was getting in and then back out of the attic—hopefully with some answers—before they came back inside. And as cold as it was out there, she did not see them staying for very long. Marie ran up the stairs and when she came to the hallway, she froze for a moment, remembering everything that had transpired up here the night before. A little shiver ran through her, now familiar to her but still unsettling. But she knew she had no time to waste, so she powered through and found the room containing the attic entrance. She felt that little pang of fear one more time as she opened the attic door and started up the stairs. She instantly felt claustrophobic and…and *what,* exactly? It wasn't anything she felt last night, though it did seem familiar.

Standing in the attic with sunlight coming in through the very same window Eva Blake had fallen out of felt strange. But the attic did seem quite different when it was exposed to the light. Now, it was almost charming—a place of idea and new visions where the room could easily be turned into anything. A new bedroom, storage, a craft room, a…

Marie turned suddenly, certain that she had heard something behind her. She shook the nerves away, reminding herself that she did not have time to jump at every single little thing. She started looking around the floor, at the neatly stacked items and boxes pushed against the wall. She understood that it was a bit naïve to think she might come across something the police overlooked, but based on every other experience she'd had in town, she thought it was more than worthwhile. She did a quick scan and found nothing. Even over by the window (now closed, obviously), there was nothing.

But once again, she was sure she heard something behind her. She wheeled around, easily picturing her own body flailing out of the window, her heart leaping in her chest. At first, she thought there was nothing there but then one of the stacked boxes tumbled from the top of its stack. It thumped to the floor anticlimactically.

As if stirred by the commotion, Marie saw a shape start to take form directly in front of her. At first, it looked like an odd assortment of dust motes making some strange erratic pattern in the air. But then she saw the edges barely visible. It was like looking at a very poorly rendered hologram, and it was something she had experienced before. She saw more definite lines and curves to the shape. Recognizing some of them—a hip, the top of a head, what looked like growing fingers.

There was a ghost in front of her, and it appeared to be materializing.

Marie quickly stepped away from the window. She slowly made her way to the stairway, not sure how the poltergeist might react. It was clear that this was one was violent and though Marie had encountered a few nasty spirits in the past, she was not accustomed to ones that sought to physically harm people. She was ready to run if necessary but also glued to the spot out of her need to get answers.

"I'm not here to run you out," she told the still-forming specter, though she wasn't even sure if this was the truth. "I just need to—"

She stopped here and more of the ghost came into view. It turned towards her, the air seeming to bend around it. Marie had no idea what to expect as even its eyes started to fill in but then when she understood exactly what she was seeing, she found it impossible to breathe.

The air grew cold. Her heart was slamming in her chest. But she knew the ghostly face looking at her and it made no sense.

"Aunt June?"

It was her; that was clear. She'd seen her aunt's ghost about half a dozen times in June Manor. But to see her here, in someone else's house, was surreal. It almost felt obscene. And even as June gave her a smile from beyond the grave, Marie couldn't help but wonder if Katie had been right somehow. Maybe she *had* somehow sent June to her house. But she had never come out and *asked* for it. Maybe, Marie thought, June had overheard her and Posey complaining about Katie and…

But was that how hauntings even worked? And if it was, did that mean…

"No," Marie said. "Aunt June…please…you didn't push that woman, did you?"

The spirit of her aunt looked confused at first and then shook her head. It occurred to Marie that she had never been able to so openly and easily communicate with a ghost before. But that was overshadowed by the weight of what they were discussing.

"Why are you here?" Marie asked. "Why did you leave June Manor?"

There was a flicker through her dead aunt's form. June seemed to tilt her head and give her a disapproving look. She opened her mouth and was clearly speaking, but Marie could not hear her.

Marie was surprised to feel the slightest flicker of fear as she stood in front of this familiar ghost; she wondered if it might just be the human mind's typical reaction when faced with irrefutable evidence of the paranormal.

"I don't know if you know what's happened here," Marie said. "and I don't know if it's *you* that has been making a mess and causing all the noise around here, but I need you to get back to June Manor."

June scowled at Marie but there was love in it. Her aunt gave a little shrugging motion and then, as if revealing some elaborate trick to a waiting audience, slowly started to disappear. Not only that, but she seemed to almost dissolve into the floor. Marie found herself reaching for June, as if she was doing nothing more than walking away.

"Wait," Marie said "June…is there something else here? Some other spirit?"

She expected no answer but she *did* hear a response. It was a sort of hushed whisper, no more than a slight breath against her ear. But it spoke a single word: *"Murder."*

With that single word, June was gone, leaving Marie alone in the attic again. Because of her unexpected encounter, Marie had lost all track of time. She gave the attic one more quick look, not sure if she had gotten the answers she was looking for at all. She thought June's odd response to her question might mean more than it seemed on the surface, and for now she had to go with that.

Confused and a little scared now, Marie hurried out of the attic, back through the bedroom, and towards the stairs. When she started walking down them, she heard her mother and Sherry speaking. They were back inside now, moving towards the large foyer and the front door beyond.

"...to understand why she doesn't quite trust Marie," Sherry was saying.

"I still think it's silly, but it is what it is," Abagail responded. "You just let her know I came by to try to mend the peace, will you?"

"I will. I think she'll appreciate it."

There was a pause here and then her mother spoke up again. She seemed uncertain, as if she might be buying some time. "Oh, and remember, if she'd be willing, we really would like the name of the guy that did the construction out on the patio."

"I'll let her know," Sherry said, her voice walking further away, towards the front door. "But I don't know if she's going to openly share that sort of information with your daughter."

Gritting her teeth, Marie quietly made her way down the stairs. She saw Sherry and her mother standing at the front door, no more than twenty feet away. Abagail had moved in such a way that her back was to the door, facing Sherry—which meant Sherry's back was facing Marie.

Marie moved as quickly as she could, staying against the half-wall by the stairs as she hurried to the back of the house. The patio doors were right there, right in front of her. She kept looking to them and turning back, looking to them and turning back, making sure Sherry did not turn and spot her. Abagail saw her and did her best to direct the conversation based on Marie's proximity to the patio doors. When she reached the doors, Abagail reached for the knob on the front door. As she turned it and opened it, Marie did the same to the patio door. And then Sherry stepped out behind her mother; apparently, though she worked for a woman that seemed to be quite cruel, Sherry at least had some form of manners, it seemed.

As Sherry stepped through the doorway, Marie opened the patio door and stepped outside. The cold wind greeted her and the nearby crashing waves seemed to applaud her escape attempt. She found the stairs off to the right, angling back in the direction of the parking lot and driveway. She reached the bottom of them and pressed herself against the edge of the house. She peered around and saw Abagail walking to her car. Straining her neck out a bit further, she saw the final second or so of Sherry walking back inside the house, closing the front door behind her.

The moment the door was closed, Marie took off at a sprint. She headed for the passenger side of her mother's car, running faster than she had in a very long time. She kept looking back to the porch to make sure Sherry had not decided to come back out. Of course, she could be watching through the foyer windows and if that was the case, this was all for naught. But as she neared the car, her mother now catching sight of her and grinning at her sprint, Marie did not see anyone looking out of those large windows.

She got into the car, slipped down in the passenger seat, and did her best to catch her breath. Abagail got behind the wheel and looked over, just as calm as you please.

"Find anything?" Abagail asked.

"Yeah," Marie said, gasping for breath. "I found that Aunt June is a prankster…even from beyond the grave."

"What?" Abagail asked, clearly confused as she cranked the car.

"I saw Aunt June in the attic."

"What? But how…I mean…why…?"

"No clue. But I think it does give us a pretty solid answer."

"What's that?" Abagail asked.

"If Aunt June has been the ghost haunting Shoreline Oaks all this time, I think we can rule her out as Eva's killer, too. I know we've been saying it was a poltergeist, but…I think it was always Aunt June. Not some malevolent spirit. And if that's the case…"

"…the killer was someone else that was there that night," Abagail finished.

They let that spoken fact settle in the car as Marie steadily got her breath back, leaving Shoreline Oaks behind them once again. She did not lose herself in the relief of it, though. She was too focused on getting to the bottom of this—and that meant returning to June Manor to see what Brendan had been able to get out of Katie Stillson.

CHAPTER NINETEEN

When Brendan returned from his lunch date with Katie, Marie could tell that he was both exhausted and rather uncomfortable. He grabbed a cup of coffee from the pot without speaking a word to anyone. When he finally made his way back to the sitting room, he let out one of the deepest sighs Marie had ever heard. She was at the check-out desk, confirming reservations for February when he called out to her.

"How did things go at the inn?"

"Um…it was interesting," she said.

She slowly made her way into the sitting room, not sure where she should even begin. As she took the seat directly beside Brendan, she could har a door opening and closing overhead. Soon after, Abagail was coming down the stairs and joining them.

"I thought I heard you," Abagail said. "How was lunch?"

"Draining. And you know…maybe I should go first. That woman loves to talk and, believe it or not, your name came up a lot," he said, looking at Marie.

"Oh, God."

"Here's the thing, though," Brendan said. "I did at least get a bit more out of her as to why she isn't your biggest fan. And it's not all about you stealing away this exceptionally daring and charming man that sits before you."

"Do tell," she said, though she was starting to brim with excitement at telling him about what she had seen at Shoreline Oaks.

"Apparently, your Great Aunt June had quite the rivalry with Katie's mother. Did you not know about it?" he eyed both women as he asked the question.

"I never even knew the woman until a few days ago," Abagail said.

"And no…I never knew about it."

"That's rather surprising, when you hear *why* they had a rivalry. It seems Katie's mother did her best to ensnare a certain man not too long after her first husband died. But that man was not having it. Apparently, when Katie's mother made her feelings known, the man shot her down. He had eyes for a certain lady—your Great Aunt June."

"Sounds like a familiar scenario," Abagail said with a grin.

Marie was slightly confused. Was all of this bitterness over unrequited loves from a present and past generation? It seemed a little silly. Then again, Katie did seem like the sort of woman that might hold a grudge.

"Not too long after that, Katie's mother moved. She's living somewhere down in Florida. And ever since then, Katie has not cared for Aunt June. So then you come along," he said, nodding to Marie, "and are essentially June incarnate. You have the same interests as June, or so it seems—all the ghost-stuff. That's how she put it, by the way. And yes…she did tell me there was a small crush on me that also heightened her anger towards you."

"She *told* you she liked you?" Marie asked.

"Yes. And rather than make your situation worse by shooting her down, I dropped the line of how I am only here for work. But…yeah, I don't think she bought it. She knows I still…"

He stopped here, as if realizing what he'd been close to admitting. He cleared his throat and smiled at her. "Wait, I haven't even told you the best part. As I told you, Katie is quite the talker. Would you like to know the man that had so won over the heart of her mother?"

"Who?" But as soon as she asked, she thought she knew. It made an odd sort of sense—and right on par with Aunt June.

"Atticus Winslow."

The laughter that came out of Marie's mouth was genuine and loud—the unexpected sort that took her by surprise. "You know, Atticus told me there was never anything romantic between them, but I wondered. Maybe it was unrequited?" Thoughtfully, and almost a little sad, she added: "It sort of makes me see him in a different light."

"Who is this Winslow character?" Abagail asked.

"Not quite as odd as Hugh Wrathe, but an eccentric fellow to say the least," Marie said. "He stayed here at the manor for about three and a half months and never came out of his room. I found out later that he and Aunt June had connected over the supernatural in the past. And while he never came out and said as much, I got the strong feeling that he once had it bad for Aunt June."

"Charming," Abagail said though it was clear she was struggling to process it all.

"So now can you please tell me what happened at the inn?" Brendan said.

"Well, my mother played her part very well, distracting Sherry so that I could get inside and up to the attic. I felt something right away, but it wasn't the same sort of threatening thing I thought I felt the night before. It felt almost familiar…and within about a minute, I saw something…"

"The poltergeist?" Brendan asked, leaning forward anxiously.

Across the room, Abagail smiled, already having heard what came next.

"It was my Great Aunt June," Marie said. "I know it sounds stupid and I don't understand *how* it happened, but she was there. And I think it goes without saying—even in death, she would not take it upon herself to kill someone."

"Are you certain she was the only spirit there?" Brendan asked.

"Fairly certain. I asked her and when she disappeared, she did not *really* give me an answer. But I swear, right at the end, I heard her say *murder.*"

Brendan was rubbing at his head and smiling. It was the look of someone that was absolutely flabbergasted with a problem, but enjoyed the task of trying to solve it. But there was sorrow and panic underneath; after all, a woman they all knew to some degree was dead. "So…it's rare, but there *are* reported cases of ghosts jumping from house to house, but it's usually only when the family has moved. This one…I don't know…it's weird."

"Do you think she could have heard us talking about how Katie Stillson has had it out for me for months and just…paid a visit?"

"Could be," Brendan said. "I've never heard of anything like it, but we can't rule it out just because we don't understand it. Hell…that's half of my job description."

"So if it wasn't a ghost that killed that poor woman," Abagail said, "where does that leave us, exactly?"

"It leaves us with a human killer," Marie said. "Which does not look particularly good for me because I was the only one with her when it happened. Not that 'a ghost did it' was ever a very strong defense."

"But you saw no one," Brendan said. "How is that possible?"

"I don't know. That house looks pretty old, right? Maybe there's some sort of hidden staircase or back entrance that goes up to that room?"

"Maybe," Brendan said. "But you'd think that would be the very sort of thing Katie would brag about. Plus…I saw that room, too. Where would there have been a secret way inside?"

"I don't know," Marie said, picturing the room in her head. "But let's say there *was* some sort of secret passage. Who would be the one to know about it?"

"Katie. But…look, I know you don't like her and she clearly doesn't like you. But all that aside…do you *really* think she'd kill someone just to make you look bad?"

The hell of it was that Marie truly *didn't* think Katie had a murderous streak in her. But for right now, it's the only thing close to an answer they had. "Even if I did think that was the case," she finally said, "I can't just go up to her and accuse her. That's only going to make things worse for me."

"So where does that leave you?" Abagail asked. She looked concerned now, the reality of the situation sinking in more than ever. With no real clues or leads to go on, she seemed to understand that the daughter she had finally reconnected with might be facing a very dark future.

"I think we need to pay another visit to Sherry," Marie said. "She was with her most of the night, right?"

"What about Wrathe?" Brendan asked.

"Maybe him, too. But the way he was moving around…I don't know. Do you think *he* could have done it?"

"I honestly have no idea. I mean…if you buy into his psychic abilities, he *may* have been able to know about some sort of secret staircase. It's a very slippery slope."

"But how do we get the two of you together?" Abagail asked. "I don't think Katie would appreciate her sole employee meeting up with you."

"It's a small town, and Sherry has been here most of her life," Marie said. "Seems like the sort of woman Posey might know a thing or two about."

With that said, Marie got up and went in search of Posey, doing whatever she could to establish even the weakest of leads to help her case.

CHAPTER TWENTY

"Oh, sure, Sherry Masterson is a sweetheart," Posey said as she chopped up a celery stalk into thin pieces. "I've known her for about fifteen years or now. Not well, mind you, but good enough. I *was* sort of surprised to hear she was working for Katie Stillson, but I assume Katie pays well. Anyway, look at me rambling. What exactly were you hoping to know?"

"I need to speak with her as soon as possible," Marie said. "And I'm sure you can imagine that I can't just pay a visit while she's on the clock at Shoreline Oaks."

"Today's Thursday, right?"

"It is. Why?"

Posey held her finger up a moment, fished her phone out of her pants pocket, and did some quick scrolling and typing. Ten second later, she was nodding as she looked at her screen.

"If you get to the library at 6:50 or so tonight, you can catch her one-on-one. Sherry's been a member of the Port Bliss Ladies Book Club for at least seven or eight years. I was on it myself at one time—but I called it a day when they started suggesting we read *Fifty Shades of Grey.*"

"And they're having it tonight, even on a holiday week?" Marie asked.

"Seems that way," Posey said, showing Marie her phone screen. The little banner she was reading said: *Ladies, bring your left-over Christmas cheer (and cookies!!!) to book club tonight!*

"Posey, you're incredible."

"Thank you. I'm starting to feel like that lonely lady in those adventure movies—the one that sits in the van and tells you what moves to make, and that you've got someone flanking you on your six."

They had a laugh over this, and it was a good feeling—a feeling that, for even just ten seconds or so, wiped away the memory of Eva Blake falling from the window, and of discovering Aunt June's ghost in the attic of her rival's bed and breakfast.

While she waited, she then thought about Hugh Wrathe. He definitely seemed like a solitary type and though she felt guilty for thinking such a thing, she was not ready to rule him out as a suspect just yet. She spent some time online looking into him and the more she learned, the more of a complex individual he seemed.

He was currently sixty-one years old and had been doing eerily accurate psychic readings since the age of the twenty-three. According to interview snippets she read about him, he first realized he could commune with the dead when his grandfather woke him up one night—his grandfather having been seven years in the ground. His grandfather had yelled at him in just a voice, not making an appearance but just an auditory presence. The message had been a simple yet important one: *"You left that damned candle burning again."* Wrathe had gotten out of bed and found that not only had he left a candle burning, but that his cat had knocked it over. Had he been three seconds later in discovering it, the flames would have reached the back of his couch and started a hellacious fire.

Over the years, he had been taken with such seriousness and credibility that the police had come to him, wondering if he could reach out to murder victims to help solve crimes. On two occasions, he'd done just that. It was those two cases that really skyrocketed him to fame. For a while, he'd had a show on television that lasted only a season and currently operated a podcast in which, one a month, he performed live, on-air sessions.

None of it cleared him of suspicion of murder as far as Marie was concerned. Sure, there was his reputation to think about, but she also wondered if maybe it was part of some promotional scheme where, in a few months, he might reach out beyond the grave to speak with the woman that had died in the same house he'd been investigating. It sure would result in a ton of podcast listens and downloads, that was for sure.

But again, she hated assuming the worst about people. She was wrestling with this very thing when Brendan walked into the sitting room while she was reading up on Wrathe. He sat down across from her and shrugged.

"I could probably get back into Shoreline Oaks, if you need to," he said. "And I don't say that just because I'm apparently the apple of Katie's eye. I say that because you saw a ghost there. Even if you *knew* the ghost…it makes me really want to get into work mode and thoroughly scope that place out. Of course…I don't think I could do such a thing while there's a pending murder investigation."

"That's okay. I'm going to see if I can't get a word or two in with Sherry Masterson in about an hour or so."

"Yes, Posey was telling me you planned to ambush her just before her book club."

"No, it's not an ambush, it's just…well…yeah, maybe it's an ambush. But just a little one." Then, quickly changing the topic, she said: "You seemed to know Hugh Wrathe pretty well. Can you tell me what your true, honest thoughts about him are?"

Brendan leaned onto the little check-in counter. Their hands were about two inches away from one another and he was close enough so that she could see the little hazel glow in his brown eyes. "He's creepy as all get out and I don't think I'd ever invite him to a dinner party. But he seems to have a legitimate gift. He's the type of man that could legitimize work in the paranormal field. From what I've seen, he does his best to steer clear of any cases or people that might smear the field."

"In other words…he likely wouldn't murder someone at a location that is reported to be haunted?"

Brendan smiled and nodded. "No, I don't think he would do that sort of thing. He might look like a ghoul but he seems to be very kind and heartfelt."

"Good to know, but it really puts a kink in proving my innocence."

Was it her imagination or did he move his hands closer to hers? She hated that she was getting hung up on such things but, at the same time, welcomed the stirring excitement. It was like discovering that first girlish crush in grade school all over again.

"I think you'll come out just fine," Brendan said.

"Why's that?"

"Because it would be a severe cosmic injustice if I came all the way out here to see you and then you end up in jail."

"But you didn't come out to see me," she said, playing along. "It was for the job, remember?"

He gave her that charming smile again and this time, he *did* move his hands closer to hers. He rested his right hand on top hers and said, "Marie…there are plenty of haunted places and spooky stories out in California."

With that and a wink, he turned away and headed for the stairs, back to his room. Marie almost asked him what that was supposed to mean but decided to leave things as they were. It was just the sort of spark she needed to motivate her as she prepared for the library to meet Sherry Masterson.

***

A cloudy winter's night had fallen by the time Marie arrived at the Port Bliss Public Library at 6:45 that afternoon. There were not a lot of cars in the lot, and the lights glowed from inside the building, casting soft little glowing squares across the lawn. Marie sat in her car, in the dark, and waited for the attendees of the book club to arrive.

She watched two cars arrive, one woman getting out of the first car and two getting out of the second. She did not recognize any of them. Sherry Masterson arrived in the next car that arrived. It was 6:53 as she got out of her car and started across the lot with a book in her hand. Marie got out of her car quickly and met her just before she reached the library sidewalk.

Sherry turned briefly, smiled politely at first, but then seemed to realize who she was smiling at. She hesitated a moment, doing an odd sort of side-step as her brain tried to figure out if it wanted to stop and address Marie or if it wanted her legs to carry her into the library as fast as they could.

"I know, I know," Marie said. "I assume I'm one of the last people you have any interest in speaking to. But please…I'm just trying to get some answers as to what happened that night."

Sherry seemed doubtful for a moment and hugged her book to her chest. "I think it's quite plain to see what happened," Sherry said.

"You're free to believe what you want," Marie said. "But the fact of the matter remains, I have to prove my innocence. I'm trying to get a complete picture of where everyone was when Mrs. Blake fell out of that window."

"Well, I'll tell you," Sherry said, glancing nervously toward the library. "You were the only one upstairs with her. As far as I know, everyone else was downstairs—particularly me."

"You never went upstairs while Mrs. Blake and myself were up there?"

"No. I was either in the kitchen cleaning up the mess than damned ghost caused, or directly beside Katie the entire time. And I know that

Brendan Peck and Hugh Wrathe saw me when it all happened. I have people that can back that up…if that's what you're looking for."

"I'm not trying to accuse anyone," Marie said.

"It is starting to seem like that."

Marie wanted to argue the point, but she supposed some of her points *did* seem a little accusatory. But at this point, she was willing to come off as being a little rude.

"Sherry…I know we don't know one another all that well. But you have to know that there's no way I would murder someone. What reason did I even have to even *consider* killing Eva Blake?"

"I don't know," Sherry said. She cast her eyes downward and shook her head. "I honestly don't *want* to believe you had anything to do with it, but given your history of getting into trouble with the law…and all the rumors about you…it's hard to ignore."

"But Sherry, you—"

"I'm sorry," Marie. I've told you everything I can and honestly, I'd rather not be seen talking to you. If I were you, I'd talk to Wrathe or Mitchell. For now, I just can't…"

"Mitchell?" Marie asked. "Who's that?"

Sherry looked at her as if she wasn't sure if she was being pranked or not. "Mitchell Powell. He was on the backside of the property when everything happened, doing some sort of panoramic experiments."

'Okay, but,…who is he? I thought we were the only ones there?"

"Mitchell is another p…you know what? No. I'm done talking to you."

Sherry stormed away and Marie let her go. It was clear that speaking to Marie made her nervous. It didn't bother Marie all that much, though; Sherry had accidentally given her another lead, as well as a mysterious bit of information. She had no idea who Mitchell Powell was, but if she had not seen him—nor anyone else she had been with—that likely meant he'd been alone the entire night. Suddenly, Sherry Masterson's side of the story did not seem so important…but finding out who Mitchell Powell was absolutely did.

CHAPTER TWENTY ONE

When Marie swung back by June Manor fifteen minutes later, she entered the house like a force of nature. Abagail and Brendan were in the sitting room, Abagail drinking tea and reading while Brendan was reviewing some of his scant footage from the night before. She took three large strides into the sitting room and pointed at Brendan. He looked up to her, wide-eyed and grinning.

"Why do I feel like I'm in trouble?" he said.

"No trouble. Well…maybe not. Do you know a guy named Mitchell Powell?"

"I do. Not on a friendly basis, but a vague professional one. Why?"

"Did you know he was out at Shoreline Oaks last night?"

Brendan closed the lid on his laptop and sat forward with great interest. "No. But how's that even the case? We would have seen him and…."

"And what?" Marie asked, still standing in the entrance of the sitting room.

"Powell is a bit unique," Brendan said. "He really only involves himself in cases where he thinks there might be a chance the house is giving off some sort of kinetic energy."

"I don't know what that means."

She could see Brendan's brow furrowing a bit as he thought of how to best address it before going on. When he did, she spoke slowly, choosing each word carefully. "There are some paranormal researchers that believe the chance of a house being haunted has nothing to do with what occurs in the house, but is all reliant on the house itself—if it carries negative energy, or maybe if the ground on which it was built has some sort of traumatic history or is built on certain lines of latitude and longitude."

"Okay…?" Marie said, wondering just how many fields of paranormal research she was still unaware of. There seemed to be no end to it as far as she was concerned.

"Mitchell is one of them. I've never worked on the same case as him, but I do know that he spends a lot of time *outside* the house rather than *inside*. So if he was there, maybe that's why we missed him."

"But why wouldn't she tell us there was another researcher there?" Marie asked.

"Well," Abagail said, also glued to the conversation, "Brendan and Eva had no idea they had both been called. And I think Wrathe was a surprise to everyone, too. It seems she was trying to keep secrets from everyone."

"But why?" Marie asked.

"The paranormal community is tight knit," Brendan said. "But many are also very competitive. I'm sure Katie probably figured that out when she started making calls. I feel pretty sure that if Eva Blake had known Wrathe was going to be there, she may not have come. Maybe she just didn't tell anyone that she had others coming. It's a crappy move on her part, but a smart one."

"I need to speak with Mitchell Powell," Marie said. Still standing in the entryway, her tone indicated that she meant *now* rather than later. She was on edge, growing very anxious, and it was evident in everything—even her voice.

"I can maybe make that happen," Brendan said. "I have his number, though he and I haven't spoken in about eight or nine months. If he's still in town, I think he'd likely meet with me."

"That would be perfect," Marie said.

Brendan pulled his phone with a speed that indicated he was starting to feel some of the pressure and excitement of the potential lead. When he placed the call and put the phone to his ear, the house seemed eerily quiet. She could hear Posey clinking and clattering around in the kitchen, but it sounded distant and almost muted in the heaviness of the moment.

The silence was broken when Brendan's call was answered. The room was so quiet that Marie could hear the muffled *"Hello?"* from the other line.

"Hey, Mitchell," Brendan said. "A little birdie told me you and I were both in the little town of Port Bliss, Maine, at the same time. Would you happen to still be around?" There was a pause here, muffled words from the other line, and gentle nodding from Brendan. "Yeah, I can do that. Sounds like fun. See you in a bit."

Brendan ended the call, se this laptop aside, and got to his feet. “He’s at the Lamplighter Pub right now,” he said. “He invited me out to have a drink or two.”

“I notice you didn’t mention me,” Marie said.

Walking to her and grabbing his coat from the rack by the door, he smiled and said, “Looks like Katie isn’t the only one keeping secrets from people, then.”

***

The Lamplighter Pub was a bit too extravagant-looking to be considered a pub in Marie’s estimation. The place looked more like a lounge of sorts, the kind of place writers and artistic types might come to share ideas and a pint. Soft ambient lighting seemed to breathe from every table, and the bar that sat large and heavy up front looked like it had been taken from the side of some long ago sea-faring vessel.

Marie and Brendan found Mitchell Powell sitting at the bar, alone. He was scrolling through something on his phone with one hand and gripping a glass of amber-colored beer in the other. He looked to be slightly younger than Brendan, maybe in his early thirties or so. He wore what Marie had always thought of as Clark Kent glasses, a button-down shirt with an abstract print, and a pair of jeans. His black hair was swooshed back with gel, giving him an almost suave sort of appearance.

He smiled a bit when he saw Brendan but when his eyes landed on Marie, he gave a concerned look. By the time Brendan was taking the barstool beside him, Mitchell was rolling his eyes.

“I think I sort of already knew you’d be bringing her,” Mitchell said. “I’m not surprised, just a little upset.”

Marie hardly knew the man so wasn’t too offended by the rude comment. She was beginning to understand that most people in the paranormal community had *some* sort of an edge to them, anyway.

Ignoring him completely, Brendan said, “Marie, this is Mitchell…Mitchell, this is Marie.”

“I’ve read a lot about you,” Mitchell said, nodding to Marie as she took the available stool on his other side. “Actually, about the *both* of you. You guys trying to start up some weird paranormal dating service or something?”

"Hardly," Brendan said. "Though I guess we do owe our bit of history to the paranormal." He paused here, as if sensing where it was headed and getting a bit uncomfortable with it.

In the silence, the bartender—a cute twenty-something woman that seemed to recognize Brendan—came over to take their orders. Brendan ordered a beer, and Marie opted for something a bit stronger than her usual glass of wine, thinking maybe a nice gin and tonic might help settler her nerves a bit.

"Mr. Powell," Marie said, "were you invited out here by Katie Stillson?"

"I was. And if I'm being real with you, I don't know how I feel about speaking with you right now."

"And why is that?"

"Well...the way I hear it, you're prime suspect Number One in Mrs. Blake's death, isn't that right?"

"Well, it's not *wrong*," Marie said. His lack of care or tact was starting to irritate her, but she kept it in check as she went on. "But with all due respect, that comment is coming from someone that was there that night and seemed to be hiding the entire time. I didn't even know you were there until one of Katie's employees told me an hour or so ago."

"That was by Katie's design. She knew what I specialized in and when she called me, I was interested right away. As I'm sure you both know, this area is a hotspot for paranormal activity. And that led me to believe it might have something to do with geography or geology. When I arrived yesterday, no one else had showed up, but she did reveal to me that she'd invited some others: our esteemed Mr. Peck, Eva Blake, and even Hugh Wrathe. I saw no point in adding to the mix inside so, because I was mostly interested in the house and the land anyway, I chose to set up outside."

"You were there the entire night?" Marie asked.

"Oh, I was there long before you and Brendan got there. I do believe Mrs. Blake arrived before I did, though. Katie came out to speak with me while Mrs. Blake was getting settled in her room."

"Where did you set up at?" Brendan asked.

"On the eastern side of the lawn, in the little grove of trees over there just before the coast takes over. It gave me a great view of the house."

"What sort of readings were you taking?" Brendan asked.

"The usual. EVPs, heat signatures, even had a little spirit box session set up and ready to go but, because of the way things turned out, I never got the chance."

"Get anything?" Brendan asked.

"I haven't really gone over the stuff yet. I think I—"

"I hate to break up the shop-talk," Marie said, "but I really need to get back to the topic."

The bartender brought their drinks over and Brendan started sipping on his right away. Mitchell turned to Marie and frowned. "Well, it seems to me that you're angling for one of two things: you're either trying to figure out where I was to see if maybe I killed her, or if I saw who did it. That about right?"

"Yes, that's pretty close," Marie said.

"Well, I hate to point all the suspicion back on you, but I've already spoken with the police. I have more than enough footage and recorded data to prove that I never left that little strip of trees. Not until after the cops got there, anyway."

Marie felt deflated in that she was already feeling this potential lead turn to nothing—but also relieved in that there was now one additional source of potential footage that might clear her name.

"Well out of that footage, did you get any sort of glimpse of what might have really happened?" Marie asked. She was holding her gin and tonic but suddenly wasn't sure if she even wanted it.

"I'm not comfortable giving you this sort of information," Mitchell said. "I was asked to hang around for a few days while the case was sorted out and I don't want to meddle."

"It's not meddling," Brendan said. "Look, Mitchell. I know you and I don't know one another all that well. But I'm telling you right here, right now, as clear as day: Marie Fortune is not a killer. We're just trying to see if there's any sort of evidence that could free her."

Mitchell took a long sip from his beer. When he set it down, he looked back and forth between them with a sad expression on his face.

"I'm going to have to disappoint you there, then, too," he said. "From where I was set up, the angle is a little off, but I *did* indeed get a shot of Eva Blake falling out of that window. But then, about four seconds after she falls, there's a very clear shot of you, Marie. You come to the window, look out for a bit, and take off running. So let's say I *did* one hundred percent believe that you had nothing to do with it…well, it wouldn't matter. That footage is pretty damning."

"And there's nothing else?" Brendan asked, his voice quiet. "Nothing else at all that shows someone coming in or out of the house?"

"None. Once Hugh Wrathe shows up, there's no one that goes inside or outside of that house until Eva Blake falls out of the window."

Marie felt fresh avenues of fear coiling up in her stomach. She could feel her chances of being freed from this case dwindling with every word out of Mitchell's mouth.

"Did Wrathe know you were there?" Brendan asked.

"No. And as far as I know, he still doesn't. Once the police questioned him, he retired to his room and that's the last I saw of him."

"I imagine they'd ask him to stick around, too."

"Oh, they did," Mitchell said. "I caught a glimpse of him this afternoon. He's staying at the same hotel I'm in too. No offense, Mrs. Fortune, but I really did not think it would be a great idea to stay at your place in light of how things went down at Shoreline Oaks."

"Nope, I get it. There are only two hotels in Port Bliss. Which one are the two of you staying at?"

"The aptly named Port Bliss Point," he said. "Nice place, just not as roomy as I'd hoped."

"Do you know if he's still there?" Brendan asked.

"You know Wrathe as well as I do, I suspect," Mitchell said. "He's not the type to get out and socialize. If the police have asked him to stay put, I imagine that's exactly what he's doing. Sitting alone, in his room, doing that Zen-zone-out thing that he does all the time." He sipped from his beer again and shook his head. "I probably shouldn't have told you any of that. So If it comes up…"

"We won't let him know where we got the information," Marie said. She then took her drink, still not having taken a single sip of it, and slid it over to him. "Consider it yours. And thanks for the info."

Brendan, realizing that they were about to be on the move again, took another sip of his beer and paid the tab, tossing a twenty dollar bill down on the bar. "Thanks again, Mitchell. Hopefully we'll all come out of this with something to show for it, huh?"

"Maybe you," Mitchell said, defeated. "Based on the bit of footage I've seen from my recordings, there's nothing to see."

"Nothing at all?"

"No. And that's another reason I'm not willing to just openly believe the death was of a supernatural cause. Based on everything I've seen about that property, I just don't think it's haunted."

Marie nearly said: *But I saw cupboards and doors flying open.* She kept it quiet though, knowing it was Aunt June that had done those things. Probably just trying to stick it to Katie for all of the problems she'd been trying to cause.

In the end, all she said was, "Thanks again." She and Brendan left Mitchel Powell alone again, just as he had been ten minutes before.

"You believe him?" Marie asked as they got back outside to the frigid parking lot.

"I know you don't want to hear it, but I do," Brendan said. "Based on the little bit I do know about Mitchell, he's an honest guy *and* never misses an opportunity to boast about recent findings or discoveries. If he had any sort of footage that would point to supernatural activity or anything out of the ordinary, he would have told us."

Getting behind the wheel of her car and cranking it to quickly get the heater going, she asked: "Do you think Wrathe is the same way?"

Brendan chucked nervously and shrugged. "I have no clue. No one in the entire paranormal community has ever quite been able to peg down Hugh Wrathe. Even in interviews, listening to the man talk is like trying put a puzzle together. Those outside of the community think he does it so all of his answers remain vague and can't be officially discredited."

"And what do *you* think?"

"I think his abilities are legit, but I think he might be a bit off his rocker."

Marie returned his nervous chuckle as she pulled out onto the street. "In other words," Marie said, "he seems like a fitting addition to this case and absolutely worth talking to."

She headed west, a bit away from the ocean, to do just that.

CHAPTER TWENTY TWO

The older gentleman at the front desk looked up from his Kindle when Marie and Brendan entered the front office. Brendan didn't even give him a chance to ask questions before he was leaning on the desk and turning on the same charm he displayed for cameras for pre-taped segments and interviews.

"I'm looking for a man named Hugh Wrathe. He told me he'd be staying here but never gave me a room number. I was hoping you could tell me if he even showed up at all."

"He did, but I can't really give out room numbers."

"Well, that's a shame. We're coordinating on a television show and we're on a tight deadline."

The old man cocked an eyebrow at him and said, "One of them ghost shows, right?"

"That's right!"

The clerk nodded and gave a thin smile. "I thought you looked familiar. Peck, right?"

"That's right, sir. Good to be noticed. Brendan Peck."

"Wrathe is in Room 37," the old man said. "But you didn't hear it from me."

Marie was a little shocked at the ease in which they got the information. She wondered if it had something to do with the sudden interest in the paranormal Posey had pointed out on Facebook. Did enough people now know about the explosion of paranormal activity in the area over the past year or so? Were more people now aware of the stories and the history and now saw it as something of a cultural benefit rather than something to be scoffed and laughed at?

Whatever the reason, it allowed Marie and Brendan to approach Hugh Wrathe's hotel room door at 8:05. Brendan seemed hesitant to knock at first, so Marie did it for him. They could both hear a heavy sigh from the other side of the door, followed by something shifting and a single, heavy footstep.

"Yes?" Wrathe called from the other side of the door. "Who's there?"

Brendan answered, doing his best to sound calm and casual. "It's Brendan Peck. I was hoping we could get together and compare notes from the investigation last night."

They were met with silence—about ten seconds of it before there was any sort of response. When it came, it came in the sound of the door unlocking and a chain being slid away from the door. It opened slowly, in a way that reminded Marie of a crypt slowly opening up in some cheesy horror movie.

Wrathe peered out at them and frowned. "You failed to mention your partner was here, too," he said.

"Well, I wasn't sure you'd open the door if I added that detail," Brendan said.

"I have no quarrel with Ms. Fortune."

"I appreciate that," Marie said.

"I suppose you want to come in?"

"That would be nice," Brendan said.

Wrathe gave that heavy sigh again and opened the door to let them in. At once, Marie noticed that he was dressed just as he had been at Katie's house. He still wore the suit and his mostly-white hair was in disarray. In a way, he reminded her a bit of Atticus Winslow, only Wrathe had more of a funeral director quality to him.

The next thing she noticed was that all of the lights in the room were off, but there were more than enough candles to create suitable lighting. Wrathe had set a series of books and notes in the floor, creating the shape of a U. A single pillow sat in the center of it all. As Marie and Brendan entered, Wrathe took a seat on the pillow and looked up to them.

"I was about to begin my evening mediations," Wrathe said. "So I would greatly appreciate it if we could wrap this up as quickly as possible." He eyed Brendan with a bit of skepticism and said: "Though you said you wanted to compare notes, I see no notebooks or computers."

"We sort of wanted your take on another part of last night."

"I figured as much. But I hate to tell you that I saw nothing. I was sitting on the back patio when I heard Mrs. Blake screaming—falling."

"And you were by yourself?" Marie asked.

"I was. I was in a deep state of concentration, listening to the interplay of the ocean and the energies surrounding the house, trying to tap into any presence that might be there."

"Did anyone *see* you alone?" Marie asked. "Did you let Katie know where you were?"

"No. As part of my agreement to visit the house, one of my stipulations was that I would be granted full privacy. No one was to speak to me unless I asked a question. I know how it seems, of course, but complete silence and isolation is often key to my success."

Marie knew she was about to take a nosedive straight down a very deep, dark rabbit hole, but she couldn't *not* ask. "Did you find anything?" she asked. "Any evidence of a haunting?"

"I felt…something. But it was not the dark and malevolent force Mrs. Stillson believed it to be. What I felt was an almost pleasant presence. I felt it only briefly but it was enough. I felt a very light sense of joy…of a childlike mischief. I was not frightened of it but, rather, wanted to explore it further."

Marie instantly thought of coming face to face with Aunt June up in the attic when she'd gone back to investigate for herself. Wrathe's description certainly seemed to line up with the ways Marie had known June in her afterlife form.

"Did the presence try to contact you in any way?" Marie asked.

Wrathe narrowed his eyes art her and then spoke to her like she was an ignorant child. "It doesn't exactly work like that. Though I suppose someone that has more or less stumbled into the paranormal community may not understand that. It's more like a give and take…allowing myself to be used as a transmitter of sorts."

"Fine then," Marie said, irritated. "Did you receive any transmissions?"

He now rolled his eyes at her and then looked to Brendan. "If this is how you two plan on conducting yourselves, you can go ahead and leave right now."

"Well then, let's be one hundred percent real with you," Brendan said. "We're here because we're trying to figure out just how Eva Blake fell out of the window. The theory among the police and about half of the town is that Marie pushed her out of the window. But I can promise you that's not the case. Not at all."

"Oh, I know that," Wrathe said.

Marie and Brendan shared a perplexed look. It was Marie that was finally able to ask: "You know *what?*"

"That you did not push Mrs. Blake."

"But if you didn't see anything, then how…"

"I see in more than one way," Wrathe said. "Whatever presence I felt, it gave me this warm, secure feeling. And in it—as *part of it*, I should say—I felt that it was trying to point me towards you and your mother. Without words, I was told you were safe…that you could be trusted and were there that night for the right reasons. I have felt similar sensations hundreds of times in the course of my career and it has *never* been wrong."

"I don't suppose you told the police about it, did you?" Marie asked.

"Don't be foolish. Something like that doesn't exactly sway courts and police. And though I felt you were very much innocent, I can't afford to throw my hat to anyone's side in matters like this. I have a reputation to think of."

Marie wanted to get furious with him, but she understood it. If he went to the police and aid he knew without a doubt that Marie had not pushed Eva because some presence or energy within the house and communicated it to him, it would not hold up *and* it could cause a ding in his reputation—especially if the end result of this case was Marie being formally arrested for suspicion of murder.

"And how do we know you didn't do it?" Brendan asked, a bit curt.

"Mrs. Masterson saw me, moments after Mrs. Blake fell from the window. I am quite old and can't move at that speed. Even a young person couldn't have, I don't believe. I'm sure the police record would back this up if you choose to investigate further."

Brendan seemed satisfied with this, though he was still clearly bothered. "Come on," he demanded. "There's got to be some truth you can stretch for Marie. All you have to do is say you're fairly certain she wasn't even—"

"No, Brendan," Marie said. "I'm not going to have him risk his reputation. I know I didn't do it, you know it, and so does my mother. And apparently, so does Mr. Wrathe. For now, that has to be enough." She then looked to Wrathe had gave a tired little nod. "Thank you for your time, Mr. Wrathe."

She started for the door, and Brendan fell in slowly behind her. As she reached for the knob, Wrathe spoke from behind her. His voice was soft and almost respectful.

"The presence I felt…you know who it is, don't you?"

He paused for a moment. An odd feeling passed through her—as if Wrathe was somehow looking into her head and sifting through her memories and knowledge.

"Yeah, I do," Marie said.

"I believe they were there for you in some odd way," Wrathe said. "I can't quite make sense of it, but that's what I keep coming back to. Whoever it is…I believe they had very strong feelings for you. Maybe you can take that in place of my unwillingness to stretch the truth for you in terms of your case?"

Marie could only nod as she finally opened the door and stepped outside. Tears stung her eyes as she headed to the car, and she wasn't quite sure why. She supposed it was because June's care and love for her was so strong even in death that someone else had bene able to feel and confirm it. Nearing the car, Brendan hesitantly reached for her hand, she let him take it. They walked to the car in silence, but somehow communicating more than words could in that moment.

Another lead had fallen through and she was afraid she may have to resort to desperate measures to clear her name this time. The complexity of the visit with Hugh Wrathe left both of them in an awkward and thick silence on the way back to June Manor. But the one thing that kept cycling through Marie's head was that she was now out of leads. Aside from trying to convince Katie Stillson to sit down with her and compare a play-by-play of the night, she was currently out of options. It made for a strange sort of feeling as they returned to the manor. There was also the fact that they'd held hands for most of the ride home; she tried to tell herself it was nothing, that she was trying to make a big middle-school deal out of it. But it was the first sign of real intimacy between the two of them since Brendan had showed back up in Port Bliss and she thought it might be more important than she was giving it credit for.

As Marie parked in the driveway and stepped out into the night, she looked up to the porch and saw that her night was far from being over. She'd been so wrapped up in the past few hours that she had missed the familiar vehicle sitting to the right of the driveway. As they walked toward the porch together, she saw the face that she associated with that little truck.

Robbie Dunne was coming out of the front door, muttering a goodbye to someone inside.

CHAPTER TWENTY THREE

She saw Robbie's face perfectly in the little sliver of light coming through the front door as he closed it behind him. When he turned to face the driveway, he spotted Marie and Brendan. She felt awful for a moment, as the disappointment at seeing Brendan was abundantly clear. But it was more than disappointment; there was hurt and genuine surprise. Apparently, whoever he'd been speaking with inside had failed to mentioned that Brendan was in town.

Trying to keep things from getting as awkward as possible, Marie acted as if there was nothing out of the ordinary about Robbie stopping by. He had, after all, been doing exactly that on occasion not too long ago.

"Hey, Robbie," she said. "You remember Brendan right?"

"Of course," he said. As they met at the stairs, the two men shook hands. Despite Marie trying to keep things as normal as possible, the tension was so thick on the stairs that Marie thought she could literally feel it pressing against her. "Sorry if I'm interrupting something," Robbie said.

"No, just coming back from meeting with a friend," Marie responded.

"Good. I was just…well, Marie, I was hoping you and I could have a second to talk."

The tension was growing thicker now. In fact, Marie had no problem imagining it having grown legs and kicking her in the backside. "Sure," she found herself saying. "Come on back inside and let's talk."

They started up the stairs, but Brendan stopped. "You know," he said, "I think I might head back to the Lamplighter and see if Mitchell is still there."

Marie turned to him, frown inching its way across her mouth. "You sure?"

"Yeah. I'll be back soon." Marie wasn't sure if he said this last bit for her benefit or as a sort of not-so-subtle message for Robbie.

He turned and walked back towards the car and for a paralyzing moment, she wasn't sure how she felt. She was, at first, rather angry for Robbie's presence but there was a softness about the way he just sort of *showed up* that was warm and familiar to her. She watched Brendan for a moment more before turning to face Robbie.

"How long have you been here?" she asked as they walked up the stairs.

"Maybe half an hour. I heard about what you're sort of stuck in the middle of with Katie Stillson and wanted to come by to see you." He opened the door for her and looked back out to the driveway where Brendan's headlights were turning around to head into town. "Maybe I should have called first."

"It's okay," she said as they stepped in together.

"So I spoke with your mother," he said. "She told me…well, she told me quite a bit, actually."

Unsure how to respond to this (and a little unnerved as the idea of how much her mother might have revealed) Marie said nothing at first. She walked into the sitting room with Robbie at her side. Abagail and Posey were seated next to one another, sipping wine. Their eyes grew wide and slightly amused when Marie and Robbie entered.

"Need the room?" her mother asked with a bit of inuendo to her voice.

"No, we're okay," Marie said. She grabbed Robbie by his sleeve and led him out of the foyer and down the hall. They branched off, heading to the new wing. It still had that new construction smell, a promise of things to come; the three new rooms that would finally be housing guests as of January 2nd. She came to a stop at the little center area, with its two benches and ornate rug.

"Again," Robbie said, taking a seat on one of the benches. "I really am sorry if I broke up any sort of plans. But…I guess the situation does make it easy for—and almost expected—to ask if you two are a thing again."

It was a question she had not dared ask herself, so it was easy to answer. "I don't know *what* we are. He's in town for a job and came by to see me. He's been sort of a sidekick through all of the nonsense that came about at Katie Stillson's place."

"That's why I'm here, like I said. I just wanted to make sure you're doing okay. This is…what? The fourth time something like this has happened to you?"

She giggled nervously, shaking her head. "Try sixth."

"My God, Marie. Is it…" He stopped here, clearly struggling for words. "I told you I spoke to your mother while I was waiting for you," he finally continued. "She told me quite a bit about this gift of yours. And if all of it's true, I think you barely scratched the surface with all that you told me about it."

"I kept some stuff to myself, yes," Marie said. "I was afraid it would scare you off."

"That's sweet of you, though a bit confusing."

"Why's that?" she asked.

"Well, you sort of ended things with me. I get it and I respect it and, honestly, I thought I was okay with it. but then when I heard that you'd gotten yourself into trouble again, it drove me a little crazy. I know it sounds a little macho and whatnot, but I wanted to check on you. I wanted to know you were okay. And it opened my eyes to the fact that maybe I wasn't as okay with you ending things as I'd hoped." He stopped and looked at her, sizing her up. "How bad is it this time?"

Her heart ached at hearing him open his heart in such a way. It was even worse now that she knew she did not feel the same. It was not guilt, but an actual pain for Robbie—a yearning for him to find what he wanted and knowing she could not provide it.

"It's not looking great," she said. "All of the leads that would have cleared me all check out. And in terms of evidence…there's none against me, but there's none to free me, either."

"A woman was pushed from a window at Shoreline Oaks, right?"

"That's the story. And I was the only one in the room with her when it happened, or so it seems."

"She didn't just *fall* out?" Robbie asked.

"I suppose that's for the police and the coroner to decide. But so far…no. They believe she was pushed."

"Is there anything I can do?"

"I really don't think so. I *will* say that it means a lot that you came by to check on me, even after I sort of shut you out."

"Forgive me for asking such a pointed question," he said timidly, "but do you think it's going to *remain* shut? Do you think at some point, there might be a future between us?"

She genuinely considered it for a moment and when she did, she came to a stark realization that she had not been expecting. She adored Robbie and thought he was easily one of the nicest, most sincere men she had ever met. But the idea of sending Brendan back to California after this trip and potentially reuniting with Robbie made no sense to her. And it made no sense because she could not accept the idea of Brendan leaving again. And just like that, without any warning or deep, personal insight to lead her along, she realized that she wanted to be with Brendan. More than that…she was pretty sure she loved him.

"I'm sorry," she said. "You've been one of the better parts about Port Bliss, but…no. Robbie, I'm so sorry."

"It's okay," he said and she could tell that he was hurt but meant it. "I just need to know you're okay. Some of this stuff your mother told me about this talent that seems to run in your family has me a little spooked. I mean…how are you not terrified all of the time?"

"I honestly don't know," she said with a laugh. "I guess I'm just used to it by now."

"And you're not in any danger, right?"

"No. The only danger I'm in right now is the possibility of going to jail for murder." Saying it out loud sent a spike of dread trough her.

Without pausing or asking for permission, Robbie stepped forward and gave her a hug. She allowed it and even sank into it a bit. "One more question," he said, his voice soft against the side of her face. "I know this gift of yours is for real now. There's no way your mother could speak about it with such enthusiasm if it wasn't. But what will you do with it? After all of this trouble in Port Bliss that you've encountered…how do you allow it to still be a part of you?"

Marie pulled away, a bit rocked by the question; it was a good one, and one she had not dared ask herself yet. She'd never even really considered what it might be like to try drowning it out. She'd been so focused on trying to understand it and how to use it that she'd never even thought about simply ignoring it and letting it go stagnant. After all, it had not become a part of her until she came to Port Bliss. It was almost like the town had activated the power, or gift.

"It might be too late now," she said. "I think it's just a part of me now. And I think I'm okay with it."

He nodded, finding it hard to look at her as he got up from the bench and started making his way back down the hall. Marie followed him and as she did, she could feel a short chapter of her life coming to a close. She knew that once he left, Robbie would be just a distant face she passed from time to time in town—and the man that owned the diner that offered up the best hot chocolate in the state.

She walked him to the door, noting that her mother and Posey had relocated, apparently sensing that this goodbye was on its way. Boo had taken their place, though. He was resting on the rug and barely looked up when they passed by.

"Thanks for checking in on me," Marie said. "It really does mean a lot."

"Take care of yourself, Marie. I'd wish you good luck with this latest scuffle with the police department, but I've seen you work it all out before. I can't help but think everything's going to be fine."

I'm not so sure about that this time, Marie thought.

She watched him walk down the stairs, back out to his truck. She hated to see him go so dejected, but at the same time was secretly happy that his visit had helped her to realize some truths she'd been fighting back about Brendan—truths that, quite honestly, she did not think she was ready to face just yet.

She toyed with the notion of heading out to the Lamplighter to find him…to speak to him and see where, exactly, they stood. Had she pushed him too hard and far away? Was there still a chance there?

But for some reason, the idea of it made her anxious and nervous. And that, piled on top of the police investigation, did not help at all. So instead of going out to find him or waiting up for him, Marie opted for something resembling a retreat. She didn't even seek out Posey and her mother, not wanting to dissect everything that had just transpired between her and Robbie. Instead, she went to her bedroom and got ready for bed. She knew she would not fall asleep anytime soon, but that was fine. She figured she could spend an hour or so in the dark, staring at the ceiling and trying to process her feelings about Brendan, the police investigation into Eva Blake, and the future—hoping that future did not include a lengthy stint in prison.

She kept thinking of the attic at Shoreline Oaks, wondering if she had missed something. If June had been there, maybe there was a reason for it. Maybe she had been trying to tell her something. She held on to that thought has sleep gracefully washed over her, hoping it would be just as clear in the morning.

CHAPTER TWENTY FOUR

Marie had no idea when she'd fallen asleep, but she was stirred awake by the sound of distant laughter from the kitchen. She peered at her alarm clock and saw that it was 7:10 in the morning. Somehow, she'd managed to sleep for more than ten hours—a luxury she had not had in quite some time. She found herself instantly wondering when Brendan had come in and if he'd been disappointed to find that she'd already gone to sleep. That also made her wonder what Brendan's plans for the day might be. She got out of bed quickly and ran to the shower. As she scrubbed and washed her hair, she replayed the meetings with Mitchell Powell and Hugh Wrathe last night, trying to find some sort of hidden nuggets that might help free her of suspicion. But there was nothing at all…which led to thoughts of Brendan and the conversation she suddenly wanted to have with him quite badly.

As she was slipping into her jeans, there was a knock at her bedroom door. She felt a bit immature when she found herself immediately hoping it was Brendan. Would they get to have that conversation already? Would they end the day back together or, at the very least, willing to discuss it?

Yet when she answered the door, she found her mother standing there. She looked concerned but was trying to hide it. "Good morning," she said. "I hate to bother you so early, but you've got a visitor. And if it goes well, I need you to tell me how things played out with you and your gentleman last night."

"Nothing played out, Mom," she said. "It was hard, and it was…well, eye-opening, I guess."

"First things first," Abagail said. "Sheriff Miles in in the sitting room."

That's not good, Marie thought as she felt the floor of her heart drop out. "How long has he been there?"

"About five minutes. When I told him you hadn't come out of your bedroom yet, he almost thought about leaving, but he said it was important."

"That's probably not good."

"I don't know," Abagail said. "He seems…I don't know…peaceful? I don't know if that's the word I'm looking for or not."

Marie had no idea what any of that could mean and figured it was a waste of time to stand there, guessing. "Tell him I'll be there in a second," she said.

Abagail nodded, her face slackening a bit as she apparently picked up on Marie's concern. When Abagail headed back towards the sitting room, Marie rushed back to the bathroom, ran a comb through her hair and did her best to look as if she had not just woken up and stepped out of the shower. She didn't bother with makeup because it was, after all, only Miles.

She headed out towards the sitting room, wondering if Brendan was up and moving round yet. She wondered if he'd reconnected with Mitchell Powell; she wondered who many drinks he'd had and if he was still sleeping soundly upstairs. But when she came to the sitting room and saw the way Miles regarded her, she momentarily forgot all about Brendan.

"Good morning, Sheriff," she said.

"Hey there, Marie. Sorry if I woke you."

"Oh, I'd been awake for a while. Is everything okay?"

Miles looked as if he might get up from his seat for a moment but then decided to stay seated. He looked up to Marie with a bit of worry and uncertainty on his face—both of which looked heavy on Miles's usually stoic face.

"A few things, actually," Miles said. "I've been speaking with your mother for a few minutes. She was very candid about this ability of yours…this *gift.*"

Marie turned to her mother and sighed. *First Robbie, now Miles,* she thought. *Are you* trying *to get me run out of town?*

Apparently seeing the tension in her stare, Miles said, "No, don't go getting upset. The thing of it is, I've always sort of *suspected* it. But I didn't want to believe it. But I guess, based on the way you've pulled yourself out of one sticky situation after another for the past eight months or so, it sort of makes sense. Now, she also told me that June is still lingering around here, in this very house, and I'm not too sure how I feel about that, to be honest. I've never seen a ghost and the mere idea of it gives me the heebie-jeebies."

"All that aside, though, there is something else I need to speak to you about. And Abagail, you may want to stick around to hear this, too."

"What is it?" Marie asked, sensing the edge in his tone.

"I'm coming here this morning as a friend, not a cop. And if this conversation ever comes up in the future for some reason, I'll flat out deny it. Listen…so far, it's looking like there is going to be absolutely nothing to go on with this Eva Blake case. Nothing new anyway. We're working to get some footage from a guy named Mitchell Powell that was filming from outside of the house. He wouldn't give up his footage without a fight, so that's a whole process we have to go through. But as of right now, all we have is at least two people claiming you likely pushed Eva Blake out of that window. So unless something comes up in the next twenty-four hours or so, you become not just a *clear* suspect, but the *only* suspect. My hands are going to be tied on this unless something new is revealed. You'll be brought in on suspicion of murder and very likely charged."

"Oh my God," Abagail said. She tottered on legs like taffy and fell into a nearby seat. Marie, on the other hand, felt as if she were rooted in place. She looked to Miles, trying to keep her panic away.

"There's *no* evidence?" she asked.

"None. None that plainly points the finger at you and none that gets you off clean, either."

"I see…"

"Now, while I'm here as a friend, I'm going to say this one more time. The hints are buried in there, and I can't just come out and say it because of this badge on my chest. Unless something new comes up, you're in trouble. Unless someone happens to stumble upon some evidence that you're innocent," he said, nodding towards her, "things could start looking very bad for you."

Marie nodded, getting the message loud and clear: he was essentially telling her to go out looking, and he would not get in her way. There was an odd and unexpected feeling of trust and gratitude that passed between them in that moment—something that had been growing slightly more and more over the last few months but had now matured.

"I understand," Marie said.

Twenty-four hours, Marie thought. *In other words, if I'm going to manage to clear my name again, I have to find something no later than tonight.*

"Good," Miles said. The expression on his face changed as he got up from the chair. With a hesitant grin, he looked around the room nervously, his eyes landing on Abagail first and then traveling to Marie. "Is June here right now? Is she here…in this room?"

"She sort of comes and goes," Marie said. "If she *is* here right now, she's choosing to stay quiet."

Miles laughed, but there was very little humor in it. It was as if he was trying to decide if Marie was being serious or not. "Well, I'll leave you to it. If things don't change, the next visit will be as the Sheriff and not a friend."

"Thanks for the heads up," Marie said, walking him to the door. Boo jointed them, trotting in from the kitchen to sniff Miles's shoes.

"Was your mother telling the truth about him, too?" Miles asked, bending slightly to scratch Boo behind the ears.

Marie chuckled and gave the sheriff an earnest sort of look. "Tell you what: if I manage to make it out of this nasty pickle, you and I can have a few drinks one day and I'll tell you everything. For now, though…I guess I need to get to work."

Miles stepped outside and gave her a quick wink. "Work?" he said, already turning his back on her. "I have no idea what you're talking about."

Miles headed down the porch stairs without looking back a single time and though he had given her permission to go looking on her own, Marie could not help but feel an ominous sense of dread as she watched him leave.

CHAPTER TWENTY FIVE

When she went back to the sitting room, she saw that Brendan had been standing on the stairs during Miles's exit. He looked shaken, apparently having heard enough to get the gist. The look of concern on his face made him look older somehow. Seeing him standing there, Boo climbed halfway up the stairs to meet him, tail wagging.

"None of that sounded particularly good," Brendan said.

"I know." She waited for him to come down the rest of the stairs before she asked: "Did you reconnect with Mitchell?"

"I did. Had a few drinks, talked shop. We spent a good amount of time talking about the ghost stories coming out of the coasts of Maine over the last century or so." He grimaced a bit when he asked his next question. "How's Robbie?"

"He's okay. He may not be very happy with me this morning, though."

"Oh?"

"Yeah. We talked about where he and I were…if there was a future. I told him I didn't see one. What I didn't tell him was that during that conversation, I think I made a pretty big decision about my future, though—of what I want it to look like." She looked into his eyes, taking his hand in hers. She knew what she wanted to say but it was terrifying. Her tongue seemed locked in place, but she managed to loosen it from the floor of her mouth. She was shaking when she finally got it out. "There can't be a future with him because I want a future with someone else."

Brendan opened his mouth to respond but was interrupted by a soft noise to the left—the clearing of a prying throat. When Marie turned, she was not at all surprised to see Posey standing there wither phone in her hand. Her cheeks were red with embarrassment as she realized what sort of moment she had just interrupted.

"Sorry," Posey said, "but I thought you should see this. I 've heard bits and pieces of it all morning…what you may be facing. And Katie Stillson only appears to be making it worse." She offered her phone to Marie, already having a certain Facebook post pulled up.

Marie took it and saw that it was a rather lengthy post that had been added forty minutes ago. She stood there with Brendan beside her, her heart sagging with every sentence she read. The latest update Katie Stillson had posted said:

By now, most of you have heard what occurred at Shoreline Oaks two nights ago. And by now, I'm sure most of you have formed your own opinions about what REALLY happened. As for me, I KNOW what happened. I was there, and I saw it. I will obviously not name names because that's called slander. However, everyone reading this knows who was here and knows who is being accused of MURDER on MY property. The fact that this person is still roaming free around town is an injustice and a smear on my business. Here's hoping swift justice will be served as this person is arrested and charged! Oh! And that mean-spirited ghost? The one I've been posting about? It seems to mysteriously have disappeared now that this has all happened. So maybe this un-named person DID have something to do with the haunting after all! So...until this is all sorted out, here's my view

"Jesus, does she think she's in the Old West or something?" Brendan asked, reading over her shoulder.

"It also seems like she's putting the Port Bliss PD on blast," Marie said.

"Which, let's be honest," Posey said, "is both a shitty *and* a smart move. "Because if the State Police get involved, you're as good as guilty. You know that, right?"

"Yes, I do," Marie said, handing the phone back to Posey. She was so distraught and despondent that she didn't even think to be angry at Katie Stillson. She could be angry later. For right now, she needed to figure out how to clear her name. And as of right now, she was coming up empty.

"How can I help?" Posey asked.

"How can *we* help?" came another voice as Rebeka stepped into the sitting room. Abagail stood beside her, nodding. Boo sat between them all, looking around in a semi-circle at the worried humans towering over him.

"I don't even know," Marie said. "I mean, we've questioned everyone we can think of and it's all coming up zeroes."

"What about that Wrathe character?" Abagail asked.

"We spoke with him last night," Brendan said.

"And another investigator that Katie had hiding out in the woods," Marie added. "And it call came to nothing."

"What about Sherry?" Abagail asked. "She was sort of zipping around all over the place, wasn't she?"

"She was…"

"I saw her running around outside for a while, dashing back and forth by the kitchen window."

"Did you ask her about it when you spoke with her?" Marie asked.

"Lord no! The last thing I wanted to do was seem confrontational."

"Well," Marie said, already heading for the front door and reaching for her coat, "fortunately I don't have a problem with that. If she was outside by herself, surely she saw *something.*"

"Didn't you already speak to her, though?" Posey asked. "Just before her book club?"

"I did. But at that time, I didn't have this little nugget of information. And the clock to my eventual arrest wasn't ticking quite as loudly."

'Hold on," Posey said. "Marie, you can't just go rampaging up into Shoreline Oaks. Katie Stillson is going to take every advantage she can. You going over there all mad and suspicious of one of her employees is a recipe for disaster!"

"She's right," Brendan said. "Be smart about this. There has to be another—"

Someone knocked on the front door and every single one of them jumped. Rebeka even had to stifle back a little shout of surprise. Curious and a bit scared, Marie reached out for the knob, turned it and opened the door.

When the person on the other side was revealed, Marie could hear Posey muttering "Oh my God," behind her.

Sherry Masterson was standing on the porch. Marie knew it was a ridiculous thought, but she couldn't help but feel that their talking about her had summoned her somehow. It wasn't too much of a stretch; when your life started to revolve around all things paranormal, there was no telling what might happen, Marie supposed.

"Hey," Marie said. She wasn't sure why, but the anger she'd felt just ten seconds ago had started fading away. Maybe it was because there was very obvious confusion on Sherry's face.

"Hi, Marie," Sherry said. "I was wondering if I could come in...maybe have a chat?"

Marie looked behind Sherry, making sure it wasn't some sort of ambush by Katie. When it was clear Sherry was alone, Marie stepped aside and said, "Come on in."

Sherry stepped inside and paused for a moment, taken aback by the sheer number of people standing in the foyer. She clearly recognized Brendan and Abagail, giving them little nods as she closed the door behind her. Marie led Sherry to the sitting room and then, after some thought, waved everyone else in as well.

"We were just talking about you," Marie said. "We were all trying to figure out a way out of this mess and your name came up."

"It did?" Sherry asked.

"Yes. My mother says she spotted you darting back and forth by the kitchen window that night."

Sherry looked genuinely confused at first and then slowly nodded. "Katie asked me a few times to check on the guy that was perched out in the woods—Mitchell Powell. She just wanted to make sure he was still there, but told me not to bother him. I know a few times I passed by the kitchen window…"

"Is that what you came to chat about?" Marie asked. She could tell Sherry had something on her mind but wasn't quite ready to rule her out as a suspect based on the excuse she'd just given.

"Not exactly," Sherry said. She looked away from Marie and then awkwardly to all of the others standing by the sitting room entryway: Rebeka, Posey, Abagail, Brendan, and even Boo.

"Sorry," Marie said, noting Sherry's unease. "With the clock ticking, we're sort of a team right now. Any chat you and I have is going to have to be in front of them."

Sherry looked uncomfortable with this, her gaze especially locking up in Abagail. "Fine, okay. I came by to speak with you because of Katie's irresponsible Facebook post. I know she's in this weird and angry place right now, but she's throwing you *and* the police under the bus. And I don't think she understands just how bad it's going to make her look in the end. But, being that *I* can see it, I wanted to come to you and clear the air. I thought about going to the police but thought I'd come to you first."

"What's in the air that needs to be cleared?" Marie asked.

"I told the police—and your mother—that I was by Katie's side the entire night. But that's not entirely true. I *was* by her side for most when I wasn't out checking on Mitchell Powell. But there was also a stretch of about five minutes when I left her side. And it might have been the most crucial five minutes of that night."

"So you lied to the police?" Marie said. She was a bit surprised at this, but her anger overruled it. This woman's lies might very well be the reason she was still being considered a serious suspect.

"I did. Katie told me to stick to her story or she'd fire me. And…I hate to say it but Katie has helped me through so much. I'd be in a very bad place if it wasn't for Katie and the job she gave me at Shoreline Oaks."

"So what happened?" Brendan asked. "Why were you not by Katie for those five minutes?"

"About a week ago, on Christmas Eve, as a matter of fact, I was alone in Shoreline Oaks. I was in the kitchen, making some Christmas punch, when I felt like I was being watched. It was so creepy that I stopped messing with the punch and stepped out of the room. I stated to feel cold…chilled to the bone, in fact. I convinced myself I was being absolutely ridiculous and walked back into the kitchen and when I did…the spoon I was using to stir the punch went flying across the room. It did not accidentally fall off of the counter; it was *pitched* across the room. It hit the wall and clattered to the floor and then it *spun.* I'm not sure what happened after that because I ran out of there so fast I almost fell down the porch stairs. I was scared out of my mind. So when Katie told me she had some experts and specialists coming to the house to check things out, I wanted no part of it. I wanted to be as far away from that house as I could be if people were coming to stir up whatever force is at work in that house. But when I told Katie, she insisted that I be there. She wanted more people she thought she could trust. So I came…"

"But?" Marie said, urging her on.

"When all of those drawers and everything started coming open in the kitchen, I panicked. I freaked right the hell out. I told Katie I was leaving. She and I had quite the spat when you guys went upstairs," she said, nodding to Marie. "Katie begged me to stay. She told me to go out to my car and just relax…take some time to calm down and then come back in. So that's what I did. I went to the car for a second, did some deep breathing. And that's when Eva fell out of the window."

"Did you see it happen?" Abagail asked.

Sherry nodded, clearly upset at the memory of it all. "I did. And when I ran up to see what the hell was going on, Katie looked…I don't know. Kind of out of her mind. And she stopped me right away and told me to tell everyone that I'd been with her the entire time. She said if I varied in my story at all, she'd fire me."

"I don't get that," Marie said. "It was already evident that she was nowhere near the attic when it happened. Right?"

"I thought so," Sherry said. "But if that were the case, why make such a request?"

No one in the room had an answer. Even Boo seemed stumped, his head resting on his paws.

"I can't figure it out," Sherry said. "And I know you don't have much time before this all comes crashing down on you, Marie. So I wanted to let you know what really happened on my side of things that night. And…to let you know that between five and six o' clock this afternoon, no one will be at Shoreline Oaks. You know…if you wanted to swing by and sort of peek around."

Marie nodded, understanding just how much trouble Sherry could be in if Katie or the police knew that she was here with them, admitting to such things. She wasn't sure if it would help much, but it was better than nothing.

"Thank you, Sherry."

"Of course," she answered, already heading back for the door. "And if you do decide to head out to Shoreline Oaks and can't find a way in, maybe check around the flower pots on the patio."

The moment the last word was out of her mouth, Sherry hurried to the door. She did not so much as turn and wave when she made her exit. She closed the door a bit too hard behind her and they all listened to the sound of her rapid footsteps down the porch stairs.

"Anyone else want to comment on the timing of her arrival?" Rebeka asked.

"Yeah, that was pretty creepy," Marie admitted. She looked around the room, not sure what she was looking for. Even if Aunt June had have showed up, she was sure there were *some* laws of nature even disembodied spirits could not manipulate.

"Seems like a sign to me," Abagail said.

"I'm not sure I believe in so-called signs," Brendan admitted.

“So? That doesn’t mean they don’t exist.” She then looked to Marie with motherly concern pasted to her face. “So what do we do now? What comes next?”

She looked to her watch a bit impatiently and said, “A visit to Shoreline Oaks. I think I might head over there around two or so.”

CHAPTER TWENTY SIX

Marie pulled her car into the driveway of Shoreline Oaks at 5:11 that afternoon, making sure she got there after Katie should be gone, according to Sherry. She'd thought about parking some distance away so her car would not be seen by any random visitor. But with everything on the line—including her likely arrest the following morning—she thought such a minor detail was worth overlooking. Besides, why take the chance of being caught on foot? It was simply a risk she was willing to take in the moment.

After parking, she did just as Sherry had suggested. As the afternoon darkened into dusk, Marie made her way onto the patio. There were eight flowerpots along the back, all barren because of the winter. She looked inside of them and then under them, finding a spare key to the back door under the one farthest to the right. When she unlocked the door and stepped inside, she truly felt out of place. She was in enemy territory, looking for answers that could potentially keep her out of jail. It felt very *James Bond* in a strange way.

She hurried upstairs, through the hallway, trough the secondary bedroom, and then into the attic space. When she came to the top of the stairs, she hesitated for a second. Dusk had the place looking like a strange crypt of some kind and it was all too easy to imagine a ghost coming out from behind the boxes, bins, and neat stacks against the wall. Seeing those stacks, she hurried over to them. She wasn't sure *what* they could be hiding, but it was certainly worth checking.

She carefully pushed and pulled, clearing the stacks and piles away from the walls. She got nothing for her efforts. All she found were dust bunnies and grime. She pushed everything back against the wall, making sure it was exactly the way it had been before she'd arrived. As she pushed the final box back, which had been sitting on top of two others and positioned by a strange painting of an alien-looking seashore, she accidentally nudged the painting. It was quite large—about three feet tall—and when she bumped into it, she feared it was going to fall from the wall and break its frame. She caught it just in time, though. And when she did, she saw the peculiar flaw in the wall behind it.

If living in June Manor for these past several months had taught her anything, it was that any sort of oddity in a wall was absolutely worth looking into. She slid the painting over even more and saw that the flaw in the wall was a smooth, thin horizontal line. It came to a point and then started traveling downwards. It looked enough like some sort of hidden doorway for Marie to remove the painting from the wall. It was quite heavy and she nearly dropped it before propping it up against some of the boxes.

With the painting removed, she realized that was *exactly*_what she was looking at: a hidden passage. A recessed grip was installed along the top, the iron of it old and scarred. The door itself had been painted the same color as the walls but looked brighter in the weak light of dusk, having been hidden for however long the painting had been there. She recalled seeing the painting on the wall when she and Eva had come up here that night, but given everything that had happened she'd naturally paid it very little attention.

Marie reached up and grabbed the handle. She pulled, and nothing happened. But when she gave it a push downwards, the section of wall slid down. She could hear metal runners somewhere below, hidden by the wall. The section of wall—a little less than three feet if she had to guess, slid downward and stopped just shy of the recessed handle that disappeared behind the wall. Marie looked down into the hole in the wall she'd just revealed and saw nothing but darkness, though she did smell an earthy scent that reminded her of an old cellar.

She grabbed her cell phone out of her pocket and shone it down the hole. She could not see the bottom, but she did she what looked like runners and an odd looking track on the back of the wall, about four feet or so farther back. There was also a single cable, running down into the darkness, hovering roughly halfway across the black gap between the opening and the wall. She turned her head and the flashlight upwards and saw a simply pulley system about two feet over her head.

"I'll be damned," she said, and the words echoed down the shaft.

She'd just found a secret elevator. Or, based on the size of the doorway and the passage, not an elevator, but a dumbwaiter. The prominent question was: *where does it end?* Certainly there had to be an exit for it because the cable led down to *somewhere.*

Marie checked her watch and saw that it was 5:40. According to Sherry, she had at least another twenty minutes before Katie would arrive home. She drew the door back up and replaced the painting where it had been. She then hurried out of the attic, retracing her previous steps back through the place. When she reached the bottom of the stairs and was standing at the cusp of the larger sitting area near the patio doors, she took a moment to re-orient herself. If the shaft had been running along the left side of the attic, she assumed the only place for it to open up would be somewhere outside—on the opposite side of the house Eva Blake had fallen from. But she recalled the cellar-like smell. She did not think there was a primary entrance to a basement on the main floor, so maybe, she supposed, there might be on old-school cellar entrance outside somewhere.

She hurried to the patio to head outside and look around when she heard a noise that froze her in her tracks.

The front door had opened. In her panic she turned around rather than bailing out of the patio doors. And when she did, she found herself staring at Katie Stillson. They locked eyes across the open space of Shoreline Oaks that sat between them and neither of them said a word at first. The tension in the air was thick enough to be felt, and Marie felt like a gunslinger, waiting to see who would be the first to draw.

It was Katie that broke the silence, taking a very purposeful step out of the foyer and towards the rear sitting area. "Are you adding breaking and entering to your murder charge?" she asked.

Marie took the key out of her pocket and shook her head. She knew she was technically in the wrong here, but could not let that stop her. "I didn't break in," she said. "You just need to hide your key in a better place."

"Fine. Trespassing. I can get you for that just as easily. What the hell are you doing here, Marie?" Marie had never seen the woman so angry.

"Looking for answers. Katie, you *know* I didn't push Eva out of that window."

"Yet that's what everyone in town is thinking. Especially the police. Oh…and speaking of the police, you should know they're on their way."

Marie felt a momentary flash of terror. Was this it? Was this how this was going to end, with a trespassing charge to throw on top of a murder charge? "What?" Marie asked, unable to contain her nerves. "What do you mean?"

"When I saw your car in my parking lot—and you weren't even in it—I assumed you'd done something stupid like this. So I went ahead and called them. Sheriff Miles will be here any moment."

"Where's your cellar, Katie?" Marie said.

The question seemed to stump Katie for a moment; she'd clearly not expected such a response. "What?"

"I found the dumbwaiter upstairs," Marie said. "I know there's another way in and out of that attic."

"What dumbwaiter are you…"

But before she could fully answer, Marie took her chance. If the police were really on the way, she didn't have much time. She sprinted to the patio doors and opened them. Katie gave chase, but she hadn't even crossed half of the space along the open-plan first floor by the time Marie was heading down the stairs on the left side of the house.

Her eyes instantly looked to the edge of the foundation and she saw what she was looking for right away. She saw the raised flower bed first. Another sat beside it, but they were both broken apart by a beautiful old cellar door. The flowerbeds hid the strange obstruction of the house's beauty. From the driveway and the parking lot, no one would have suspected there was a cellar door there.

Marie reached for the door handle but saw the padlock that sat closed between the handle and the clasp. Not that it mattered…by the time she realized she wasn't getting into the cellar, she saw Miles's patrol car pulling in and parking behind her car. And when he got out and came walking across the lawn with officer Creighton in town, he did *not* look happy.

CHAPTER TWENTY SEVEN

"What are you doing here, Marie?" Miles asked.

She knew she couldn't mention his visit to June Manor earlier that morning. She could only hope he had that visit in the back of his mind as the next several minutes played themselves out.

"I was desperate," she said. "I came here looking for answers."

"The call we got from Mrs. Stillson says you were trespassing. That you broke into her house."

"I used a key."

"Did she give you this key?" Miles asked.

She felt panic rising up in her. She had really not thought this through very well, had she. She's always known there was a chance she'd get caught, but how had she not considered the possible repercussions? If she finally ended up heading to jail after all she's been through because of Katie Stillson, she might very well lose her mind.

"No," she said. "But I found it on the patio."

Miles placed his hands on his hips and sighed. "But did you know that Mrs. Stillson would not want you in her home? Were you snooping around somewhere you did not belong?"

"Yes."

Creighton looked over to Katie, who was looking like she had just won the lottery. "Mrs. Stillson, to the best of your knowledge, did Ms. Fortune break or steal anything?"

"No. I'm not sure what she was doing. Probably up in the attic to make sure she didn't leave any evidence behind."

"Is that what you were doing?" Miles asked Marie.

The panic was momentarily flushed away by anger. Katie wasn't wasting any time trying to once again place all of the blame and guilt on her.

"I was in the attic, but not looking for evidence," Marie said. "Well, not *that* kind of evidence, anyway. I did find something, though. I think it's a dumbwaiter or some sort of service elevator…another way in and out of the attic."

A look of vague interest crossed Miles's face as he looked over to Katie. "Why did you not mention this on the night?"

"Because there isn't anything like that in my house!"

"The entrance is hiding behind a painting in the attic," Marie said.

"That's ridiculous," Katie bellowed. "I think I'd know if there was an elevator shaft in my house!" Marie studied her in the waning dusk and thought she might be telling the truth. She wasn't sure what this meant, but…

"It's there," Marie said. "I saw it. I looked right down into it. And I'm guessing the other end of it is in this cellar."

Miles and Creighton shared a look before Miles then cast his eyes upwards toward the attic. When he finally looked back down to the cellar, he then looked to Katie. "Mrs. Stillson, where is the key to this lock?"

"Inside on one of my keyrings."

"Would you mind fetching that key and letting me have a look inside?"

"Of course," Katie said, determined.

"Officer Creighton, would you please accompany her?"

Creighton nodded, though it was clear she was puzzled by the order. Katie did not seem to like it, either. She scowled, but said nothing as she and Creighton headed for the patio stairs. Miles and Marie remained silent until they could hear the patio door closing.

"Maybe this is my fault," Miles said. "I *knew* I shouldn't have come by this morning to basically let you loose on this thing."

"Why would she lie about a dumbwaiter being there?" Marie asked.

"I don't know. I'm wondering, though, if she legitimately didn't know. It's a stupid lie to tell…something that can very easily be proven false."

"You don't think she did it?" Marie asked. Even as the question came rolling out, Marie wasn't quite sure herself. Katie had truly seemed shocked over the news of the dumbwaiter. It seemed impossible at first, but then again she had no issue with assuming Katie was the type of woman that had been *very* hands-off during the rebuild and remodel of the place.

"I'm not ready to say that just yet," Miles said. "But right now, I'm looking for any available answer I can find. Much like you."

"There's more," Marie said. "Sherry Masterson visited me this morning. She said—"

"She said Katie threatened to fire her if she didn't tell one particular story. Yes…we know. She came to us not too long after she came to you. It's a damning bit of evidence which we fully intend to consider. Between you and me, I think the way this whole thing plays out right now, right here, is going to play a huge part in how this all ends."

"Yes, but did you—"

The patio door opened again. When it did, Katie apparently cut the flood lights on because the gathering darkness of incoming night was suddenly illuminated. Two shadows reached Katie and Miles before Creighton and Katie did. Katie walked directly to Miles and handed him a ring of keys with one of the keys already selected and picked out.

"Help yourself," she said.

Miles took the key from her and inserted it into the small padlock. It opened easily, and he removed the lock and swung the cellar door open.

"There's no light down there," Katie said apologetically. "it's an old cellar…almost like a storm shelter or something. I was going to get electricity down there but just didn't see the point."

Miles removed the flashlight from his belt and clicked it on. Creighton did the same and they walked down the thin, rickety steps together. When Marie started to follow him down, he called back over his shoulder: "You two stay up there."

Katie gave Marie a look of contempt as she crossed her arms against the cold. She then looked down into the cellar. Marie did as well, watching the two flashlight beams dancing back and forth.

"Mrs. Stillson," Creighton called. "What do you use this area for? Looks like just storage, is that right?"

"That's right. There's an old push mower down there, some old china I'll likely never use, boxes of magazines, things like that."

Marie could hear the two cops murmuring something down below. She could also hear them moving things around. At one point, Marie heard what she thought might be one of them gently knocking against something made of wood.

"Did you put these sheets of plywood here against the back corner?" Miles called out.

"No. It was there when I purchased the property. The guys that did the remodel said it didn't make sense to touch anything up down there if I wasn't going to use the space, so I just told them to leave it. They thought it might be hiding something structural."

There was more commotion form down below and then what sounded like something heavy falling over.

"What's wrong?" Katie called down, stepping closer to the cellar entrance. Marie could see clear signs of worry on her face.

"Both of you come down here," Miles said. "Slowly, and one by one."

Katie went first, basically shouldering Marie to the side. Marie went next and the women both walked down into the darkness. The creaking of the old wooden steps seemed to greet them. Marie had been in plenty of dark, creepy places recently but it still affected her. She felt the darkness sliding over her, as if it was hugging her and did not want her to leave.

Marie followed behind Katie, finding that the glow of the two flashlights did a decent job of filling the cellar. It was about ten feet by fifteen feet. The floor was made of a thin and well-work layer of concrete and the walls were a combination of old cinderblock and reinforced wood. Marie assumed they were currently under the primary, smaller sitting room on the first floor.

As soon as her senses got accustomed to the layout, she heard Katie gasp in front of her. "What in the hell?" she asked.

Against the far wall and located in the corner, Miles had pulled away a sheet of plywood. Where it had previously been, there was a small door about two feet off of the ground; it looked exactly like the one Marie had found up in the attic, only this one was dustier and more beaten up. As the women walked even closer, Miles reached up to the recessed handle and pulled down on it.

The car to the dumbwaiter sat inside. It wasn't much at all—just a wooden platform outlined in metal, with slatted iron bars on the sides. The back was mostly open, revealing the track installed into the wall behind it.

"And you didn't know this was here?" Miles said, looking directly at Katie. "You still want us to believe that?"

"I swear, I didn't," Katie shouted. There were tears spilling form the corners of her confused eyes. Marie was torn in that moment. She was quite certain that the reveal of this dumbwaiter might help to clear her name, but she was also equally certain that Katie had truly not known about its existence. This opened up a whole new well of possibilities.

“This plywood has recently been torn down,” Miles said. He kicked at one of the corners, showing where it had been damaged, the entire corner splintered and broken. “When I just now took it down, it was clear that it had just been propped up.”

“According to Ms. Fortune, there’s a painting upstairs on the attic wall,” Creighton said. “We’re going to go have a look in a second, but would you like to confirm that for us right now?”

“Yes, there’s a painting…”

“And you’ve never moved it?”

“No! It was here when I bought the place, already on the wall. I thought it looked so odd that I just left it there and…and…”

“You may also want to know,” Miles said, “that someone else came to us today--someone else that was here the night Mrs. Clark died. Katie…did you demand that Sherry Masterson say she was with you the entire time?”

Marie saw the shift in Katie’s eyes. In the blink of an eye, she’d gone from indignant accuser to subtly accused. There was fear and despair in her eyes, made even more apparent in the ghostly light of the flashlights.

“Mrs. Stillson, we’re going to head up to the attic,” Miles said. “I want you to come inside with us and wrap up your day however you need to wrap it. After that, I’d like you to come down to the station.”

“What? Am I…am I under arrest?” There was a tremor in her voice and Marie thought she saw streaks of tears in the glow of the flashlight.

“Just come inside with us,” Miles said, not formally answering her question. He aimed his flashlight beam back towards the cellar steps and shook it.

Katie turned her head to follow the beam, starting for the stairs. When her gaze passed by Marie, there was ice in it. She was terrified and confused, sure, but there was fury there, too. And quite honestly, it was the first time during this crazy ordeal that Marie thought Katie Stillson might actually be capable of murder.

CHAPTER TWENTY EIGHT

Marie returned to June Manor, feeling colder than the temperature outside warranted. The quick transition in the cellar—from Katie becoming the accused rather than the accuser, as well as that blood-chilling look—had struck Marie hard. She was so affected by it that she left her coat on when she entered June Manor, doing anything she could to get that chill out of her bones.

Brendan and Boo were there to greet her right away. She could tell that Brendan was trying to read her eyes, doing what he could to determine the outcome of the trip without coming out and just asking.

"Katie showed up while I was there," she said. "She called the police, but it sort of backfired on her."

Abagail came rushing in as Marie went to the sitting room and fell into Aunt June's chair. Posey and Rebeka came next. Posey looked rather comical, having been caught in the middle of preparing some sort of dessert; she held a measuring spoon in one hand, and a bag of brown sugar in the other.

"Are you okay?" Abagail asked.

"I think so. I don't think it's a case-closed situation yet, but…I think I might be out of the woods. At worst, I might get a fine for trespassing."

"Who was it?" Brendan asked.

"They're looking at Katie right now. Miles and Creighton took her to the station and—"

"Woah, woah, hold on," Posey said, shaking the measuring spoon at her. "You look shaken, sweetie. But can you start from the beginning?"

Marie nodded, finally deciding to take her coat off. "After moving some boxes around upstairs, I nudged up against this weird painting on the wall. I'd seen it the other times I was up there, but never really paid much attention to it." She then walked them through everything, from opening up the door for the dumbwaiter, to Miles uncovering the one down in the cellar. It didn't take long, and Marie found that she did seem to thaw out a bit as she told the story.

"I can't believe it," Posey said. "I mean, let's be real here: the woman has always been a class-A bitch. But I never thought she'd actually kill someone."

"Well, we don't know *for sure* she did," Marie said. "All we know is that there is now a confirmed way in and out of that room."

"And it would have to be someone that knew the house well," Brendan added.

"That's either Katie or Sherry," Marie said. "And I don't think either of them would do something like that. Or, rather, I *didn't* think they would."

"I hate to be the voice of reason here," Rebeka said, "but why don't you stop stressing over it? The police now have Katie and they know about the dumbwaiter. Even if it doesn't one hundred percent absolutely free you, it opens up more leads, right? Why not just let them do their job?"

"She may have a point, Abagail said. "Marie, there's only so much you can do. And I think you've already done far more than anyone might expect."

"They're right, you know," Posey said. "Honey, I've seen you endure this stuff longer than anyone here. It's not always your fight, you know. Sherriff Miles knows you well by now. He'd going to do everything he can to make sure you're not charged—especially with this whole dumbwaiter business."

Marie nodded, getting rather sentimental to see all of the love and support around her. She was fairly certain she could even feel something else in the room, some other form of encouragement that went unseen. Thinking that it might be Aunt June there to show her support, a tear came trickling out of Marie's left eye. She wiped it away quickly and looked around the room, taking in each loving face.

"Thanks, everyone."

"Of course," Abagail said. "What can we do for you right now? What do you need?"

She looked to Posey and smiled. "Is there a bottle of red open?"

"Always," Posey said, hurrying into the kitchen and finally realizing she was holding a measuring spoon and brown sugar.

But even as Posey went to fetch the wine, something nagged at the back of Marie's mind—some little detail that she was sure she'd missed. When she tried to grasp it, all she saw was the black hole of the dumbwaiter door, tunneling down through the walls of Shoreline Oaks like a hungry, greedy throat.

***

Sleep seemed as if it wanted to come that night, but Marie's overwhelmed mind kept pushing it away. She was too hung up on the developments at Shoreline Oaks: if Katie was really the killer, how someone might have so noiselessly used the dumbwaiter and removed the painting and *why* anyone would have wanted Eva Clark dead. But it was when she thought of the painting that she got the most hung up. She had certainly seen it before but *had* it been hanging on the wall? The more she tried to recall the layout of the room, she wondered if it had always been like that. At some point, hadn't there just been boxes covering the wall where the dumbwaiter door had been?

She wasn't sure. And just as she thought she had a grasp on that question, her brain would shift gears and focus on Brendan. She was quite sure she was in love with him and if this case did indeed end with her freedom, she thought she might ask him to stay here with her. She doubted he'd give up his new life in LA for his drama-filled coastal one, but she had to at least ask.

Back and forth her mind went, from one huge unanswered question to the next. Finally, sometime around midnight, she finally fell asleep. When she did, she landed squarely in the amorphous arms of a dream that wasn't quite a nightmare, but was far from pleasant.

She was sitting on the back patio of Shoreline Oaks, looking out to the ocean. Heavy storm clouds rolled out over the water and the water seemed to surge in anticipation of it. It looked as if something massive was moving under the water, but she could not quite make out its shape.

"Don't bother looking," a voice said from beside her. "You won't ever see it, looking that way."

Marie turned her head and saw Aunt June sitting in the chair beside her. She, too, was looking out to the churning ocean. She looked younger than Marie remembered her; June's brown hair, slightly tinged with grays here and there, whipped in the wind.

"Why am I here?" Marie asked.

"Peace, clam, and understanding," June said.

"That makes no sense."

June smiled and said, “That doesn’t mean it’s not true.”

Down below, in a small strip of grass Marie was pretty sure did not actually exist behind Shoreline Oaks, she saw Brendan and Boo playing together. They both looked up at her, expectantly.

“What do I do next?” Marie asked.

“You take the jump. But first, you need to look deeper.”

Marie looked back out to Brendan and Boo. Behind them, the clouds were getting darker, fatter. The sea was in a frenzy now, awaiting the storm.

“What do you mean deeper?” Marie asked, turning to June.

But June was no longer there. Instead, Eva Blake sat in her place. When she opened her mouth to speak, her teeth were gone and it opened far too wide. It looked very much like the dumbwaiter shaft.

“Look deeeeeper....”

Marie moaned as she sat up straight in bed. She looked around the room, fully expecting Eva Blake to be there. But there was only Boo, looking up to her with slight annoyance. He was probably getting tire of being stirred awake by his master being spooked by bad dreams.

“Look deeper,” she muttered, seeing the words come out of Eva Blake’s cavernous dream-mouth.

In the dream, the comment could have meant any number of things. But as her mind stirred somewhat awake and she could feel the reality of her bed beneath her, she thought she understood exactly what Aunt June and Eva Blake had been saying.

Looking deeper…into the murder.

CHAPTER TWENTY NINE

While winter had always been one of her favorite seasons, Marie would have given absolutely anything to be able to enjoy her coffee on the patio, staring at the ocean while feeling the sun on her skin. This was especially true after the dream she'd had last night, and the message she'd taken away from it.

Look deeper.

She was drinking her coffee in the sitting room while the movement of her family and friends filtered throughout the house. Her mother and Posey were in the kitchen, cooking up eggs and bacon. Rebeka was on the iPad at the check-in counter, looking at new rugs for the extension. Brendan and Boo were somewhere upstairs. It all felt warm and familiar. It was one of the rare moments where June Manor felt more like her home that her business.

She thought about the attic in Shoreline Oaks, trying to recall if she'd seen that painting on the wall every single time she'd been up there. She'd been so focused on finding a ghost the first time that her memory of what the room had looked like was hazy. Maybe there *had* been a different configuration of boxes, stacked a different way in which they'd hidden the door to the dumbwaiter. Maybe someone had moved it all around slightly, hoping no one would notice.

If this was true, it did seem to paint Katie in a bad light. While she'd insisted right down to the bitter end that she had known nothing about the dumbwaiter, Marie found it hard to believe. Then again, she did know what it was like to take on a house that offered up the occasional surprise. A dumbwaiter Katie had not known about didn't seem quite as hard to swallow as the hidden rooms placed all around June Manor, after all.

"You're thinking very hard about something," Brendan's voice said. He was coming down the stairs, holding his laptop. "Everything okay?"

"Maybe," she said. "I don't know. The way things played out yesterday just seems sort of unfinished."

"Marie, I thought you were going to drop this."

"I know, I know…but did you ever go up in the attic?"

"Just for a second, but that was a bit before you and Eva went in there. Why?"

"Do you remember seeing a painting on the wall?"

Brendan thought about it for a moment and then shook his head. He took the seat next to her and opened up his laptop. "I don't remember," he said. "I mean, I remember boxes stacked up nearly against the walls, but that's about it. There *might* have been a painting, but I'm not sure."

"Did you get any footage from the attic?"

"No," he said. "I was only using the thermal imager up there."

"Can it see inside walls?"

Brendan smiled, clearly liking the way her mind was working. "Unfortunately, no," he said. "Pointing it at the wall only gives me the heat signature off the wall. It sort of bounces from the surface. Sorry." He then let out a sigh and looked at her with great concern. But there was also understanding in his eyes; whatever she said next or ended up doing, that look alone told her that he was on her side.

"Are you having one of your moments of doubt?" he asked.

"Maybe," she said with a warm smile.

"Can I ask why?"

"Because I started thinking deeper. I don't know *what* I'm missing, but there's definitely something."

"So you're going to do some detective work today?"

"I think so. I just don't…I don't know. I don't know where to start."

"Well, I'm always available to help, but I need some sort of promise of job security. I can't have you fire me if I talk too much or make some sort of—"

She stopped listening here because he said something that, all at once, seemed to be vastly important. She sat up slowly, instinctively reaching for her phone though she was not yet sure who she needed to call. The idea was forming, though, and it suddenly seemed very important.

I can't have you fire me if I talk too much or…

"Let me guess," Brendan said. "I said something very profound that inspired you. Right?"

She gave him that same warm smile and when she got to her feet, allowed herself to kiss him on the cheek. She wanted to do much more than that but the idea that was now taking root in her head was all she had time for.

She unlocked her phone and pulled up a number she honestly didn't think she'd ever call again. With a sort of dawning clarity, she pressed CALL and waited for Sherry Masterson to answer the other line.

When Sherry did answer, she sounded tired and uncertain. Apparently, she had never expected Marie to call her, either. "Hey, Marie. Is everything okay?"

"For now, yes. I guess you heard about Katie by now?"

"I did. Not that it matters. She knows I ratted her out, so any friendship there is busted. I just don't think she did it. And I don't say that out of loyalty. Katie is many things, but she's not a killer."

"Well, I wanted to ask *you* something…something about the attic. How often did you go up there?"

"Not too often. I mean, when she hired me on as help, she was in the process of moving some stuff up there. I maybe went in there three or four times in the span of six months."

"Do you remember seeing that painting of the beach…looked like a beach on another planet or something."

"Yes. It was somehow pretty and ugly all at the same time."

"Every time you saw it, was it hanging up?"

"Yes. Why?"

"I have this sort of gnawing feeling…a feeling that it might not have been hanging that night. I think it was taken down and there were boxes pushed in front of the dumbwaiter door."

"The…the what?"

"The dumbwaiter. I found one yesterday. There are at least two openings, maybe more. One in the attic, and one in the cellar."

"I had no idea there was a dumbwaiter in that house. I suppose it makes sense, though. It was pretty old."

"Yeah, Katie swears she didn't know about it, either. Which, to me, seems a little unrealistic."

"I'll tell you this," Sherry said. "If she *did* know about it, she never said a word about it to me."

"I wanted to ask you something else, though. I wanted to know if you were the only employee she's had."

"I'm the only consistent employee," she said. "There have been a few people here and there, but no one long term. There was the interior designer that practically lived there for two weeks, for instance. And then there were the handymen and movers. I guess that's what you'd call them. Sort of jacks-of-all-trades, you know?"

"Did she ever have cross words with any of them?" Katie asked.

"Are you kidding? It's Katie Stillson. Of course there were cross words here and there."

"Did any one of them stand out to you?"

Sherry was quiet for a moment but then let out a *huh* sound. Even in that one single noise, Marie could tell that her voice was shaky. "I wasn't there to witness it, but I do recall Katie being really upset with one of the guys she had moving things around and doing some light construction not too long after I was hired. I never even thought about it until now. As you can imagine, it's not anything out of the ordinary for Katie to rant and rave about someone."

"Do you remember the guy's name?" Marie asked. Suddenly, her mind was buzzing. She was on the cusp now. Not only would she be freeing her name, but she thought she also might very well find the killer.

"Not right off hand," Sherry said. "Something Danielson. I'm sure she has it in her records or emails or something. If you really want, I can dig for it. I mean, do you think it's important?"

"I don't know. Do you know if he was ever in the attic?"

"Oh, I know he was. One of the reasons Katie was so angry with him and ended up firing him was because he dropped a box and ended up breaking some sort of lamp or something. And I…ah hell, Marie. He was also in the cellar a lot. Putting up plywood or drywall, I think."

Marie's heart started to slam in her chest, The connection was a clear one, but she still had no idea what it all meant. As she tried to sort it all out, she did manage to say: "Yes, Sherry. I think it's very important that I get his name."

***

"You should probably tell the police."

Brendan spoke these words to her but the tone he used indicated that he knew Marie would do no such thing. After she and Sherry had ended their call, Marie had downed the rest of her coffee and stared to pace the sitting room. She did not notice, but Boo started to pace as well. He looked alert and cautious, as if he knew they were about to head out somewhere and there was work to be done.

"That *would* be the smart thing to do," Marie said. "But I have a feeling about this one. I wish I could explain it, but it's very hard. Maybe it's because I saw Aunt June in that attic. But I think it's supposed to be me."

"If you're going to look for a man you think may have somehow had a hand in Eva's murder, I'm coming with you," Brendan said.

Another voice responded from the dining room entrance. "You'll have to fight me for it, then," Abagail said. "I've only heard bits and pieces of this whole thing and it already sounds dangerous."

"Yeah," Posey said, her head poking in behind Abagail. She could even see Rebeka standing just behind Posey, as if afraid to join the conversation. If the situation hadn't been so dire, Marie would have found the sight of her seemingly floating head quite funny. "What were you talking about with boxes and a painting?"

Marie looked around the room at each face. This was her family. It was made all the more special by the fact that her actual biological mother was here—a mother she had all but given up on. She'd come to Port Bliss with no real support, leaving a broken relationship behind and facing a future with no one. And now, less than a year later, she had more support than she could ever dream of. She loved them all and, despite the heaviness of the moment, felt incredibly blessed.

"I appreciate the concern," Marie said, meaning it. She had to fight the emotion rising up in her voice just to get the words out. "But I think I need to do this alone. I really wish I could explain it, but…"

She was interrupted by the ringing of her phone. She glanced at the display and saw that it was Sherry, calling back. Before answering it, she looked to the four faces (five, counting Boo) and smiled.

"Trust me on this, okay?"

Brendan nodded right away. Rebeka came next, and it took Abagail and Posey a bit longer to follow suit. Still, she noted the look of understanding on her mother's face before she accepted Sherry's call.

"Hey, Sherry. You got that name?"

"Barry Umbridge. And better than that, I've got an address, too. I guess it's where Katie mailed his checks."

"Thanks, Sherry." Already, she was thinking about what this might mean and how she should react. The easy answer was: go to the police. Let Sherriff Miles know. But when had she ever gone with the easy answer? If someone was truly guilty and saw the cops on their doorstep, that was one thing. But if it was her, an innocent-looking local business owner, things might go a bit differently.

"Sure," Sherry said. "But what are you going to do? Are you going to talk to this guy?"

"I think so. I think I have to."

"Okay. Just be careful. If anything happens to you, I'd feel responsible."

Marie looked back to the loving faces that were listening in and grinned. "I'll be okay," she said. "I've got a pretty great team at my back."

She ended the call and pocketed the phone. "Really guys, it's okay," she said. "You act like I've never done anything out of the ordinary and a little dangerous before."

"Two hours," Abagail said. "If I haven't seen or heard from you in two hours, I'm calling the police."

Marie thought it was a little overdramatic, but fair. "Fine. And in that case, I suppose I should get going."

She gave them all a little wave and as she headed for the door, she supposed she understood why they were so hesitant to let her go. There was something in the air, some sort of vibe that wasn't quite negative but *pressing.* She had no doubt it was either Aunt June or the house itself; whatever it was, she thought it was an indication that this was an important moment. This was not her instinct or her guts, but the very presence of June Manor and whatever supernatural forces residing inside of it letting her know that she was on the brink of…well, of *something.*

When she stepped outside onto the porch, the feeling dissipated a bit, but the sense of importance remained. It lessened as she reached the car and when she opened the door, she looked back to the house.

"I hear you," she said. "I just don't know quite what you're trying to say. If you—"

She was interrupted when the front door open. The moment it was cracked, Boo came running out. He was barking as he sped towards her, dashing across the lawn and looking at her as if he could absolutely not believe that she had been about to leave him behind. Posey stood at the partially opened front door, looking out.

"He was going nuts," she said. "Scratching and clawing at the door, whining like I've never heard before."

Already, Boo was trying to nudge his way past Marie so her could get into the car.

"You want to come along, too, huh?"

He whined as she stepped aside to let him in. He climbed across the center console and took his place in the passenger seat. He was calmed down right away, looking back to her as to ask her what was taking her so long.

She got into the car and closed the door. She looked to him and a sense of finality came over her. She did not feel in danger but seemed to feel that some part of her life was about to come to a close.

"Ready, boy?" she asked.

Boo's tail wagged lazily a single time as she cranked the car to life. As she came to the end of the driveway, she looked into the rearview mirror. She almost expected to see all four of them watching her leave—Brendan or her mother at the very least, But there was no one there.

Only…was that true?

For the briefest of moments, she thought she saw a woman standing there in the yard, just to the right of the stairs—Aunt June, there one moment and then gone the next, vanishing into thin air. It was the final motivator Marie needed to visit this man named Barry Umbridge, a man she now suspected might be the key to truly solving this mystery.

CHAPTER THIRTY

The Umbridge home sat on a stretch of road and scraggly land that had been mostly overtaken by coastal greenery and the homes of people that didn't mind living *by* the beach, just not directly on it. The yard was surrounded by scrub grass and winter-stripped crape myrtles. The house itself was rather charming, a two-story home that looked slightly modern but without any real maintenance over the years. Marie pulled into the short gravel driveway, parking behind an old eight-passenger van. A beat-up red Toyota truck was parked beside the van. A few pieces of lumber were propped against the tailgate.

When Marie got out, she peered over to the truck and saw a dented toolbox and a few scattered tools in the truck bed; it was a good match for a man that did light construction work—just the sort of man Marie had come hoping to find.

As she started for the house, Boo barked softly at her. She turned back to the car and smiled at him. "Hold tight, boy," she said. "You're charming and all, but not everyone is automatically cool with dogs in their homes."

He whined, as if this made no sense to him at all, but then sat obediently in the passenger seat.

Marie walked up onto the quaint porch. She knocked on the door, which was still adorned with a Christmas wreath. As she waited for an answer, Marie found it hard to believe that Christmas had just been a few days ago. These last few days felt as if they had stretched on forever.

Within a few moments, the door was answered by a middle-aged woman. She was wearing an apron that was lightly dusted with flour. Somewhere behind her, soft Christmas music played.

"Hey there," the woman said. "Can I help you?"

"Maybe," Marie said, taken aback by the door being answered by a woman. She even wondered for a moment if she'd heard Sherry wrong. Had she said *Mary* Umbridge? Was this woman the killer?

She doubted it, so she went ahead as planned. "I'm looking for Barry Umbridge. I was told he lived here."

"He does," the woman said with a hint of irritation in her voice. "You need to speak with him?"

"Yes, if it's not too much trouble."

"Sure. Come on in."

Marie stepped inside and smelled cinnamon rolls cooking. She felt instantly terrible, comparing them to the heavenly aroma of the cinnamon rolls Posey could whip up. They made it a few steps into the house, just inside a little living room, before the woman called out: "Barry! You've got a visitor!"

The shouting surprised Marie, but there was something almost funny about it. She assumed this woman was Barry's mother and, if so, this exchange have her a pretty clear glimpse into their relationship. The mother turned to Marie frowned. "Was it one of his piss-poor jobs?" she asked quietly. "He's been getting lots of complaints about his construction work lately. He's not quite been himself the last few months…"

"No, nothing like that," Marie said. She worried that this woman would stay by her son's side as they tried to have the conversation she already mapped out in her head. If that was the case, things were going to get very tense *very* fast.

The sound of heavy footsteps upstairs, coming down a set of stairs off to the left, filled the house. Again, the mother frowned and turned to Marie. "Have a seat. If you stick around long enough, I have some cinnamon rolls about to come out of the oven."

"Thank you very much. But I don't think I'll be here long."

"You sure it's not about one of his jobs then?" the mother asked with a knowing smile.

She then left the room and at about the same time, a young man of about twenty-two or so came into the room. He was dressed in a hoody and a pair of torn jeans. His black hair hung on his face in some sort of grungy rocker look and he had the appearance of someone that stayed up late most night—perpetually tired, with a five o' clock shadow.

He looked to Marie, cocking his head and narrowing his eyes. He looked up to make sure his mother was out of the room and said, "Who are you?"

Marie was standing just inside the living room. The young man had come in through the same entryway, but he angled himself into the corner, taking a seat in a small armchair. He was very scrawny and short-statured…in other words, more than capable of fitting inside the space of the hidden dumbwaiter in Shoreline Oaks.

"My name is Marie Fortune," she said. "I own and operate June Manor in Port Bliss. I was hoping you could maybe answer some questions for me about a woman you used to work for."

"Questions? You mean like references? You have some work you need to have done out at your place?"

"Not exactly. Listen, I don't know if you've heard or not, but there was recently a death up at Shoreline Oaks. I'm trying to figure out exactly what happened, and I'm trying to talk to any people that might have an inside knowledge of the house. I learned just this morning that not only did you once work for Katie Stillson, but that she also fired you in a rather disruptive way."

The guilt was all over Barry's face the moment she mentioned a death at Shoreline Oaks. He shifted uncomfortably in his seat and his eyes flittered about everywhere other than Marie's face. He tried to play it off but he was pushed so for back in the armchair that she thought he might pass right through it.

"Yeah, *disruptive* is a pretty fitting word," Barry said. "I mean, she was a really uptight lady from the start, you know? You pick up a box a little too roughly, and she'd lose her damn mind. But I dropped a box up there in that attic and oh my Lord, you'd think I pulled a gun on her. But…what does that have to do with anything? You said someone was murdered. Why does her firing me have anything to do with that?"

He asked it far too defensively; Barry Umbridge did not have any sort of poker face at all. While his reactions to the news and her sudden presence in his house was not nearly enough to think he was certainly guilty, Marie thought it made him a very likely suspect—much more likely that Katie Stillson or herself.

"Well, I know the woman that died," Marie said. "And the suspect they currently have…well, let's just say they aren't the killing type. What I want to know about is the dumbwaiter."

His reaction was even stronger this time. He sat up and shook his head. "Look, I worked for her and she fired me. And I think she likely also spread my name around town, sort of smearing my name, you know? I don't want to talk about her or her stupid house."

"Not even if you can free an innocent person? I just need to know what sort of shape the dumbwaiter was in when you and the other mover men used it."

She laid the bait pretty perfectly if she did say so herself. Now, the question remained if his worry and guilt would have him blindly snapping at it.

He seemed to consider something for a moment, but it was very brief. "Well," he said quickly. "It was small and that pulley system was old. We were afraid to put anything too heavy on it."

"But you did use it?"

"Yeah," he said, only the end of the single syllable was stretched out, as if he knew he had maybe just said something he shouldn't. Marie could sense a small shift in the conversation and in that moment, shew felt a surge of adrenaline. Everything was about to change; she could feel it. Something was about to happen. She could feel it in the air like an electrical charge.

Marie took the chance, knowing it was about to get very uncomfortable. "Was it you that put the plywood up over it in the cellar?"

"What?" he asked, though it was clear he knew exactly what she was asking.

"You must have done it very quickly to get out of there in time," Marie said. "I guess you were already *in* the dumbwaiter that night. Did you move the painting before everyone showed up or what?"

His eyes were wide and for a moment, she thought he might start weeping. Instead, Barry Umbridge's face seemed to calm all at once and a small smile touched the edges of his mouth. He stood slowly and the odd smile on his face caused Marie to take a step back. As she did, she hear something clattering in the kitchen as the mother moved about.

"The dumbwaiter was a trap, right? I wasn't supposed to know about it. That your clever way of getting me to confess without confessing?"

The smile on his face widened and Marie realized in that moment that not only was she standing in front of a killer, but a killer that likely didn't even care.

"So it was you…?"

Her heart felt as if it had stopped. Looking into his unforgiving eyes made her feel about twenty degrees colder, as if she's just stepped into the December ocean.

"I suppose it was," he said. "But I didn't think it would *kill* her." He was speaking low, glancing over his shoulder. "If you want to talk this out, we can. But I'd really rather my mother didn't hear about it."

She had no idea why, but the look he gave her as he said this was scarier than any moment she'd spent in a haunted location by far. She struggled to find where to go next, what words to use. And while she struggled, he mocked her.

"Go on. Tell me what you think. What do you think?"

Marie found some extra courage residing inside of her. She reminded herself that she'd faced ghosts and more uncertainty and fear in the last year than this young man had likely ever felt in his entire life. He wasn't worth the fear. And more than that, it seemed like he was the answer to clearing an innocent woman's name—even if it *was* Katie Stillson.

"The dumbwaiter was sort of hidden," she said, centering each word around the extra bit of courage. "I think you and maybe a few of the other men that were working with you might have known about it but said nothing to Katie. I think you were pissed off at being fired and spoken down to, and I think you also knew about Katie's stories around town about her place being haunted."

"Oh, that's for sure," he said. "She was crazy on top of being mean. That night, when I went through the woods and into the cellar…I was just going to make some noises and scare her." He smiled widely at this thought, then shrugged it away. "But then, I heard it all through the walls. She'd put this little ghostbusting team together and when I heard about some of them going up to the attic…well, I just couldn't resist. So yeah…when I got the chance…I gave her a little shove. Now, I didn't mean for her to actually *die.* I thought she'd hit that little overhang off the side of the patio. But I suppose I pushed too far…"

"Wait," Marie said. "You think…you think it was Katie Stillson that fell out of the window?"

"Well yeah!" Uncertainty then came over his face and that devilish grin dropped. "What the hell are you trying to say?"

"Katie was downstairs when you ushed that woman out of the window. It wasn't Katie you pushed. It was a woman named Eva Clark. And she died on impact."

"You're lying."

"I'm really not. Katie is very much alive and currently being held on suspicion of murder." What she did not add to that was: *Thanks to me…*

Barry Umbridge's eyes went wide with shock and surprise. His pupils darted left and right for a moment, as if he were literally searching for an answer. Yet as a few seconds passed, he seemed to accept it. It sank into his reasoning and his expression once again turned to an icy scowl.

"Then the way I see it, there's no problem," he said. "She'll still get what she deserves in the end."

"Life in prison because she fired you? Really?" Marie was surprised to find that she was growing angry. And with that anger came more confidence.

"That and just being an overall evil woman. You said you own June Manor right? Isn't that the same place she's always trying to tear down and put out of business?"

"Yes, but this is different."

"No. This is not my problem," he said. And then, taking another step towards her, he added: "But if you don't get out of my house right now, there *will* be one."

Marie, unflinching, pulled her phone out of her pocket. "I think a call to Sheriff Miles will make it a pretty significant problem for you, actually."

She fully intended to make the call, too—right there in front of Barry Umbridge, She figured if he wanted to try to act all intimidating, then she could dish it right back to him. But before she even had time to fully get the phone out of her pocket, Barry did something that shocked her. Maybe it was her being so naïve or being accustomed to supernatural encounters, but she had *never* even considered that he might attack her. Especially not with his mother in the next room.

But that's exactly what he did. With no warning at all, Barry reached out and shoved her. Both of his hands struck her on her shoulders. She stumbled back, her feet nearly coming completely off of the ground; scrawny-looking or not, Barry Umbridge was apparently very strong.

Marie let out a little cry of surprise as her phone went sailing into the air and Barry made a quick dash for the front door. In a move that Marie could only chalk up to instinct, she extended her leg, trying to trip him as he ran, but she just missed. He opened the front door quickly and went barreling outside. Marie scrambled to her feet just as the mother came hurrying into the living room.

"What's going on?" she asked. "Did he…did he *hit* you?"

Marie, not wanting to get sidetracked, stumbled a bit and regained her footing as she rushed for the door. With a sneer of determination, she said, “With all due respect, that’s the least of his problems.”

And with that, Marie dashed out of the front door and chased after a killer.

CHAPTER THIRTY ONE

The first peculiar thing Marie experienced as she came out of the Umbridge house was a sort of magnetic feeling that made her feel dizzy at first. She could see Barry Umbridge running hard to the right, in the direction of Port Bliss. Already, he was passing over into the neighbor's backyard. Marie turned in that direction and made it only one step before every nerve and muscle in her body seemed to pull her in the opposite direction. Confused, she peered over that way and looked to her car. Boo was now in the driver's seat, paws up on the side of the door and barking maniacally at Barry's running form.

Marie ran to the car and, again working on nothing more than pure instinct, opened the door and let Boo out. He came out like a rocket and looked back to her, as if to make sure she was coming, too. Marie did just that, following after Boo as he tried to close the distance between him and Barry. Marie reached for her phone to call the police but realized she'd left it somewhere on the floor back at the Umbridge home. So for now, she supposed, it was all going to come down to a foot chase between her and Barry—or, rather, between Boo and Barry.

By the time she had come halfway across the neighbor's back yard, Barry was already jumping over a little raised flower bed that sat between two houses. He cleared it easily, and Marie was amazed at how fast and agile he now seemed based on the lazy and lackluster first impression. While she was impressed at this, she was not all that impressed by his forethought. Even if he managed to outrun Boo, what, exactly did he hope to accomplish by running away—especially running in the direction of Port Bliss? She supposed it really didn't matter. She couldn't let him get away. If so, she was back to square one and all she had to go on was her word and theory.

She watched as Boo reached the flowerbed and leaped over it. She smiled, as it was the most active she'd seen him in a while. Of course, as Marie reached the flowerbed in question, she was just about out of breath. She couldn't remember the last time she'd run at a sprint of any significant distance. Sure, the other day she'd ran from the patio of

Shoreline Oaks to her mother's car but that wasn't exactly a long distance.

Marie wasn't able to clear the flowerbed like Boo and Barry had; she had to leap up on it, sidestepping a sad-looking aloe plant as she made her way down into the yard. A few feet ahead, she saw that Boo was closing in, right at the edge of yet another yard. Barry noticed it, too, taking a furtive glances over his shoulder. He let out a little cry as Boo closed the distance and then nipped at his heel.

If Marie hadn't been struggling for breath, she would have found the picture funny. Boo had gotten a mouthful of Barry Umbridge's baggy pants. He was tugging at them right above the ankle and pulling back, letting out growls that sounded almost playful. It slowed him enough to allow Marie to close the distance, too. She had no idea what she was going to do if she caught up to them, but she did know she would—

She watched as Barry Umbridge drew his free leg back to kick Boo. Marie knew *exactly* what she was going to do in that moment and she did not give pause. As she drew closer to them, just a few feet between them, she found herself launching herself at Barry. Somehow, she was flying, sending herself towards him as if he was some sort of football player trying to prevent a touchdown.

She had just enough time to think: *Marie what the hell are you do—* before her shoulder struck his stomach and her arms went around him. She took him down in a tackle as they both went toward the ground.

Only, there was no ground. A pool waited behind them, mostly drained and winterized. Thankfully, a black pool cover was pulled over the empty space so when they fell, it was only for a few feet before the tarp stopped them. Still, there was collected rainwater waiting for them. The shock of cold cause them both to gasp. Marie fought for purchase with Barry Umbridge beneath her. She looked up to the edge of the pool and saw Boo, looking down. He was still growling but she was also surprised to see that his tail was wagging. She hoped it was because he could sense he'd done a good job. Or maybe it was because he thought his master was playing some odd game.

Her attention as broken as Barry writhed under her. More than that, a wild thrashing hand came up and clocked her in the side of the head—not a punch, but very close to it. Marie, having never been in a physical fight in her life, did her best to retaliate. She drove her elbow in what she assumed was his chest and he yelped in response.

As they continued to wrestle about, the trap came undone from the sides of the pool. When one of the sides came falling over them, icy, stagnant water chilled her to the bone. She felt another of those wild, misplaced punches strike her low in the ribs. This one hurt quite badly but she still managed to push herself away. Instead of attempting to fight back, she got to her knees in a very wobbly position and pulled the fallen edge of the tarp over on top of Barry. He wailed as she reached down and pulled it tight. When she did, another side of the tarp pulled away from its clasps and they went falling about a foot or so to the hard concrete below. Fortunately for Marie, Barry's body beneath her softened the blow.

As she pushed herself back up to her feet against her and the slick material of the pool cover, there was another noise—a booming voice from overhead.

"Hey! What are you two doing?" an older gentleman said peering down at them from an overhanging patio. "Get out of there right now before I call the police!"

"Please do," Marie bellowed, her voice thinned out because of the frigid bit of water they had splashed into.

"Get off of me!" Barry yelled from under the wrapped portion of the tarp.

"Ma'am," the old man said, now concerned, "You need some help? Did he hurt you?"

"Call the cops! Ask for Sheriff Miles! And yes…I could use a hand if you can manage it."

Barry Umbridge managed to slip out from under the tarp. He ignored Marie completely and reached for the edge of the pool. His shoes slipped on the cover as he reached up and saw Boo standing there, waiting. Boo let out a little growl and the look on Barry's face made it quite clear that he knew he wasn't going anywhere until the police arrived.

***

As it turned out, Barry Umbridge's mother had already called the police after she suspected her son had struck a woman and there was now some sort of chase going on. The police had already responded by the time the old man with the pool—whose name was Alfred Yancy—called roughly five minutes later.

Marie was sitting in Alfred's modest living room when Miles and Creighton arrived on the scene. He'd given Marie a dry sweatshirt, a jacket, and a blanket to warm herself up. As for Barry Umbridge, he'd also been given a means to get dry and get warm. And then Alfred Yancy had promptly locked him in the bathroom from the outside.

When Miles sat down across from Marie, Barry was speaking to anyone that would listen from the bathroom. "I'm not sure how I'm the bad guy here! She sent a dog after me and then tackled me into an empty pool!"

Miles sighed and rolled his eyes as he looked to Marie and then to Creighton. "Officer Creighton, would you mind taking down his side of the story while I speak with Marie?"

"Sounds like fun," Creighton said as she started walking towards the complaining Alfred Yancy played the host very well, escorting Creighton and leaving Miles and Marie to their discussion.

"I really hope he's the killer," Miles said. "If he's not, your case is going to look so much worse."

"He's the killer, that's for sure," Marie said. "Only, I don't think he really *meant* to kill anyone. He thought he was just putting a little scare into Katie. But he confused Eva for Katie and…well, here we are."

"And he just told you all of this?" Miles asked

"Yeah. Seemed like bragging but…I don't know. There was also something a little creepy and dangerous about him."

"He hit you?"

"Sort of. It was more like a really hard push and then he was fighting for purchase when we were in the tarp."

"And do you think he'd admit the same things to us that he told you?" Miles asked.

"I just don't know. He did seem a little proud of what he'd done when he still thought it was Katie that had fallen from the window. He even—"

She was interrupted by the approaching sound of Barry Umbridge's voice. He was crying but in a sort of strained way. He still showed some of the tenacity Marie had seen in him back in his house but it was luring far behind fear and brokenness.

"…and I didn't even know it was her," he was moaning. "I swear, I didn't meant to *kill* anyone!"

"Okay, so tell us about it," Creighton said. "It's okay, Mr. Umbridge, just calm down and tell us." She guided him to one of

Alfred Yancy's chairs as Alfred looked on from the entryway between his hall and living room.

Barry looked to Creighton and then to Miles. He overlooked Marie, perhaps still not too happy from having been tackled into Alfred's pool and then locked in the bathroom.

"He says he'll talk," Creighton said. "He insists he never meant to kill anyone, especially not Eva Blake, and wants us to know the truth if we think it might help his case."

"The truth is always good, son," Miles said. "Why not start at the beginning?"

"She knew some of it," Barry said, nodding at Marie. "I was working over at Shoreline Oaks, helping to move stuff, doing some fix-up stuff here and there. Mrs. Stillson told me it would only be for a few weeks, but that was fine with me. She paid good and I needed the money. But that it is one of the meanest women I've ever met. Thinks the world just revolved around her, you know? She fired me because I dropped a box and broke something…but I also stole some things, too. She didn't know about that, though." He stopped here, as if wondering if he'd just revealed too much. "So, after she fired me, I started seeing on Facebook and hearing around town that she thought her house was haunted. So I figured I could use that old dumbwaiter to scare her, you know? Make some noises in the walls, come and go as I please…"

"She didn't know the dumbwaiter was there?"

"No. And me and some of the other guys thought it would be funny to not tell her. Even then we were joking about using it to prank her, you know. I know it sounds bad, but she was so damned *mean.* So a few nights ago, right before Christmas, I asked one of the guys I was working with if they had ever told her about it and they said they hadn't. So I went over there one night, went into the cellar and hid out. I was starting to up the dumbwaiter when I heard everyone—and realized she had some people over to hunt that ghost. When I knew the attic was still empty, I went up and took that painting down…hid the dumbwaiter door with some boxes so I could get in and out easy. I stayed up on that floor with the door cracked…"

He stopped here again and started weeping. Marie hated to hear it; she was pretty sure there was genuine regret in his voice, despite the fright he'd put into her when he'd attacked her.

"Sherriff, is it okay if I don't listen?" Marie asked. She wasn't sure why she felt the need to not hear it all again, but it was strong. *Maybe, I don't want to feel sorry for a murderer, for starters,* she thought.

"Yes, that's fine," he said. "You can sit out in the car if you want. I believe Boo is already out there, waiting for you."

Marie nodded and got to her feet. Before she left through the front door, she turned and looked to Barry Umbridge. He did indeed look like a broken man—a man that had been so challenging and scary just half an hour ago, now broken and scared. She knew he was only being so forthcoming in the hopes of getting a lesser sentence for what he had done, but something about it unnerved her.

She went outside and found the patrol car sitting in Alfred's driveway. When Boo saw her, he sat up straight, tail wagging, She got into the front passenger side and let Boo curl up awkwardly in her lap. He was trembling a bit, making her wonder if the entire ordeal had scared him, too. He looked up to her and licked her on the side of the face.

"Something's different this time," she said quietly. "You feel it, too, don't you?"

He let out a huffy breath and settled his head in the crook of her arm. She hugged him as well as she could as she looked to Alfred Yancy's house, waiting to hear the eventual outcome of yet another murder case that had somehow ended up revolving around her.

After this, she had no idea what might be around the corner. For the last few days, she'd felt a sense of things wrapping up, of a circle coming to a close. She wasn't sure what that meant—if it concerned, her mother, Brendan, something to do with June Manor…or all of it. All she knew was that the future was laid out in front of her. And if the last few months had taught her anything, there was always uncertainty and happiness around the corner, both in equal measure.

CHAPTER THIRTY TWO

New Year's Eve

Brendan's bags were packed. They were sitting in the corner of the sitting room, in the same place the Christmas tree had stood until yesterday. Marie walked into the sitting room with a cup of tea and looked at them sadly. Her heart sagged at the thought of Brendan leaving her again. It would have been a terrible moment if it had not been interrupted by a round boisterous laughter from the kitchen. It was a noise she'd heard quite a bit since after Christmas—the sound of her mother and Posey growing closer and becoming friends.

Something about the sight of his bags stirred something inside of her. It was similar to the feeling of something changing, something coming to a close. She'd felt it a few times in the last few days and was only now starting to suspect she knew what it might mean. And quite honestly, Marie wasn't sure if she was ready to face it.

She was pulled out of her thoughts by the dinging of her cellphone as a text came in. She retrieved the phone from her pocket and read the text from Katie Stillson. It read: **We still on for 9?**

She responded without even thinking, though it was already 8:45 in the morning. She typed in **Yes** and then looked out of the sitting room, to the stairs. She knew Brendan wasn't scheduled to leave until noon and as far as she was concerned, meeting Katie was the perfect excuse to avoid a very tense and awkward conversation with Brendan before he left. Marie sipped from her tea and started walking towards the kitchen to tell Abagail and Posey that she was headed out. After a single step, though, she decided not to. Her mother had already expressed her unease with a meeting with Katie and Posey would probably only re-direct her attention to Brendan. They both knew about the morning meeting with Katie, so she figured she was fine to just leave unannounced.

That's exactly what she did, getting in her car and driving down to Red Reef Diner on the last morning of the year. She was dumbfounded that it felt almost natural to be meeting with Katie after all they had been through. Katie had been released from police custody as soon as the official arrest of Barry Umbridge had been made. From what Miles had told her, he and Creighton had made it known that Marie had been responsible for her freedom. Katie had reached out right away and that very brief text conversation had led to this—a New Year's Eve meeting at Red Reef Diner.

When she walked in, there was no apprehension about running into Robbie and, to her surprise, no anger or unease about meeting face-to-face with Katie. Ever since falling into that empty pool, she'd felt differently about nearly everything…and she wasn't sure why. Her hope was that chatting with Katie would help her to figure it all out.

She took a seat and when the waitress came by, she ordered a hot chocolate. From her seat, she looked behind the counter, looking for any sign of Robbie. She saw him once and they locked eyes for a moment. He gave her a formal smile, waved, and then went about his business. It wasn't exactly closure, but she was happy that she'd seen no shock or pain in his face.

Marie was halfway done with her hot chocolate when Katie arrived. She approached the table slowly and when she sat down she looked like a woman prepared to meet a firing squad.

"I know I already texted it," Katie said, "but that's not quite the same. I had to meet you to tell you how grateful I am. Sure, there was some trespassing and all kinds of blame being passed around, but in the end it was your stubbornness that proved that I was innocent."

"In all fairness, I was trying to free *my* name first," Marie said.

Katie looked to Marie for a moment, interrupted when the waitress came by. Katie ordered an omelet and a coffee and then folded her hands in front of her when the waitress was gone. "Marie," she finally said, "I've been pretty awful to you."

"Agreed," Marie said. She offered a smile with the word, letting Katie know this wasn't going to be as hard as it could have been.

"I suppose by now Brendan has told you why I sort of came after you?"

"He did," Marie said. "And really, I rather hope your coming after me had more to do with the history of your grandmother and Attius Winslow than it did with the crush on Brendan."

"It did. You have to think…in a town like this *and* in a small family, the things a grandmother tells a grandchild are like the gospel."

"Oh, I can attest to that," Marie said.

"My grandmother *loathed* June. I know that sounds terrible, but it is what it is. And I grew up my entire life hearing it. I heard about how June swept in and stole a man away from her. Hell…I got older and wasn't even sure if there was any truth to it. But I knew you were in town and that brought it all back up in my mind. Then you throw in the timing with Brendan…"

"Did you *know* him before he showed up in town?" Marie asked.

"Just from television. But that was all it took. It's embarrassing to admit now, but…yeah. Throw all of that together and it's…well, it's why I'm here, offering a sincere apology."

"Apology accepted," Marie said. "On one condition."

"Name it," Katie said. The relief in her eyes was massive.

"No more dirty posts on Facebook. Your grandmother and my Aunt June are gone, Atticus Winslow is off somewhere doing God knows what, and Brendan is heading back to LA later today. I'd say all of that can set the grudge to rest, right?"

"Deal," Katie said. "But…I have to ask. The thing with Brendan…he's really going back?"

"Yes. I think there might be something there, but…he's got his career, you know?"

"He's got it bad, you know? When we had that lunch—which I'm now thinking was bogus and part of one of your plans—it was apparent. I think he loves you. And I think you love him. Seems like a waste to just let it go."

It was nice to have confirmation from someone else, someone that could see how he felt about her. And it was sad in a way to hear it coming from Katie. Even though her crush had been almost obsessive and she'd not handled it well, a broken heart was a broken heart no matter how you looked at it.

"I know," Marie said. "It's just too much trouble…too much work."

"I brought him out here to legitimately have a look at my house," Katie said. "But I also wanted to get to know him, too. And it all blew up in my face and here the two of you are again. Not that you asked, but it seems to me that things are coming full circle. It's like you two are *supposed* to be together."

Marie had nothing to say to that. She was too wrapped up in the *full circle* comment. Time and time again over the last few days, she felt that something was coming to a close. Maybe a close to her paranormal adventures, maybe a close to her time in Port Bliss. She wasn't sure. But with her mother showing up and then Brendan reappearing in her life, she wondered if the feeling she's had wasn't so much about things coming to an end as it was about things slowly starting…

"You okay?" Katie asked.

"Yeah, I think I am," she said as the thought took root. "Oh, and I suppose I owe you an apology, too."

"For what?"

"While I didn't send a ghost to your inn to haunt it…I sort of know the guilty party."

"What?"

Smiling, Marie sipped from her hot chocolate and started to tell Katie about how Aunt June wasn't as gone as Katie's grandmother might have hoped. But even as she revealed her secrets, her thoughts were on Brendan…and the future.

***

When she got back to June Manor half an hour later, her heart seemed to explode in her chest when she saw Brendan in the driveway. He was putting his bags into the trunk of his car. Boo was at his feet, looking up at him in a sad sort of way. Marie parked directly beside him and took a moment to compose herself before she got out of the car. She wasn't sure what she was going to say but she knew what she wanted to accomplish, and she thought that might be enough.

When she did get out of the car, they locked eyes and did not look away until Marie reached the trunk of his car.

"You trying to sneak away early?" she asked him.

"No. Actually, I was trying to avoid us having the awkward goodbye conversation as I put my bags in my car. It appears that didn't work so well. I thought we'd have lunch together somewhere. Maybe even have Posey whip something up as a final farewell."

"Do you really want to go?" Marie asked.

"No." His answer was a quick and abrupt as her question. "But the longest I could stay here would be January second, and it would just be too rushed."

She knew what she was about to say—what she was about to suggest—and it terrified her. But she'd gotten used to being scared as of late. She'd learned that from time to time, there was fruit at the other end of fear, and she hoped this was one such time.

"This car is a rental, right?"

"Yeah. From the airport. Why?"

"Leave it here. Let's go together."

"What?" he asked. He looked at her cautiously—clearly not wanting to assume what she meant. But the hope in his eyes was staggering and if she ever doubted she loved him, it was blown away in that moment.

"How long does it take to drive to California from here?"

"A couple of days, I'd think," he said. Then, grinning, he said, "Actually, it's about forty-six hours. I may have Googled it a few times over the last couple of weeks. But why are you—"

She stopped him with a kiss. In less than a second, her body felt weightless. She'd been wanting to do this since she saw him in her doorway a few days ago. She'd wanted to do this ever since he'd left for LA the first time.

When they pulled apart, there were three words on her tongue. Speaking them out loud terrified her. It was much scarier than any of the things she'd encountered during her time in Port Bliss.

Fortunately, she did not have to say it first.

"I love you, Marie," Brendan said. "I knew it when I left the first time."

"Then why did you leave?"

"That's *why* I left. I don't do the best with relationships. And you and I were just on different paths and—"

"We still are," she pointed out. "But I know I want to be with you." She took a deep breath and added: "And I know I love you, too. And I want to be wherever you are."

He smiled at the three words and she thought she saw the traces of tears in his eyes. "Even Los Angeles?" he said.

"Maybe. There are things I'd need to work out."

"Like June Manor," Brendan said, looking to the house. "Like your mother."

"Yeah, like those things. But what I do know is that the only way you're leaving here this morning is if I'm with you."

"How?"

She shrugged and looked down to Boo. He was standing beside her, tail wagging wildly. She knew it was crazy, but she got the notion that he understood exactly what was going on…what was about to happen.

"Let's go see if Posey will whip up some lunch," Marie said. "I think if we all put our heads together, we'll figure something out. My mom coming back when she did, and then you…I can't think that was just coincidence."

"But my flight," Brendan said. "I have to leave at noon. And that's pushing it."

"I'll talk to Posey about lunch. You call and cancel your flight."

"Or I could just buy you a ticket."

She shook her head and reached down to Boo. "I'm not leaving without him. We're driving. You can catch your flight if you need to, but I really don't want to drive two days alone."

This time, Brendan kissed her. It was long and deep and she didn't want it to end.

"You sure about this?" he asked her when they broke apart again.

"No," she said. "But the last time I wasn't sure about something, I moved to Port Bliss. And in hindsight, it was the best thing I ever did for myself. Now stop asking questions and let's go have lunch."

He kissed her again, quickly, and they walked back to the house hand in hand. Boo followed, weaving between their legs, barking excitedly. And when they entered the house and saw everyone already standing in the sitting room, it was clear that they knew, too—Abagail, Posey, and Rebeka all smiled widely at them. Marie was not at all surprised to see that Posey was wiping away tears.

"Spill it," Posey said. "Is he staying here or are you going to LA?"

Even before Marie said anything, Abagail stepped forward and gave her daughter a huge hug. "I always thought California would suit you," she said. And then, in a whisper that only Marie heard: "If you'll let me, I'll hold the fort down here. I think Aunt June and I have some catching up to do."

EPILOGUE

The Pacific Ocean did have a certain sort of glittering quality the Atlantic did not have, but Marie was still partial to the sunsets in Port Bliss. Still, it *was* pretty cool to know that Santa Monica was less than ten minutes away. She'd been here for three weeks now, and was sort of stunned by the sun. The scenery might be better in Port Bliss, but she'd take the California sun over the Maine winters any day.

She sat on the beach, watching the tide start to roll in. She also watched the furry shape running to her side. Boo dropped the ball she'd just thrown and looked at her, eager for her to toss it again. She did, throwing it barely into the water. She giggled at the sight of it. Even if she'd ended up hating Los Angeles, Boo liked it enough for both of them.

"You're going to run that poor dog to death," a voice said from behind her. She turned and saw Brendan walking towards her. That was another thing she did prefer about Los Angeles over Port Bliss; Brendan just *fit* here. Also, he looked damned good with a tan.

"You're late," Marie said.

"I know. I ran by the apartment to change." He smiled as he sat down beside her and handed her something. It was a large glossy square that instantly brought a tear to her eye. "This came in the mail for you."

She took the offered mail and blinked the tears away. It was a postcard. On the front was a wide, sprawling beach. In very basic Times New Roman font, the header above the ocean read *Port Bliss Welcomes You!*

Marie turned it over in and they both read the brief note scrawled on the back. As they read, Boo delivered the ball back to his owner but waited patiently. The note read:

As of next week, all rooms are booked. Between now and April 15, we have only one empty room. Rebeka has moved out and is living in an apartment in town. Posey is still Posey, cooking and chatting and keeping me from drowning. Saw Sheriff Miles in town today and he says things are awfully quiet since you've gone away. Like me, he seems to be very eager for you to come back. Soak up the sun and enjoy yourself. We'll be here when you come by for a visit. Also, Aunt June sends her regards. I suppose that's what she was trying to say...

Love,

Mom

"I'm not crying, you're crying," Marie said.

"Hey, I didn't say anything." Brendan waited a beat and then added: "But you know, if we're going to visit for a few days, it needs to be sometime before the middle of March."

"Yeah?" she asked, excitement in her voice.

"Yeah. The network loved the pitch. They want you and Boo to be an on-camera part of the spin-off. Your name *and* a dog sidekick...there's already a bidding war. But after March fifteenth, you're going to have lots of meetings and interviews."

She hugged him and they both fell over in the sand. Boo sniffed at them to see what was wrong, his tail wagging the entire time.

"You sure you're okay with me intruding on your spotlight?" she asked.

"I'm sure. I don't mind you intruding on much of anything."

They shared a kiss and then resumed throwing the ball to Boo. They took turns, throwing it until the sun was nearly hiding completely behind the ocean. From time to time, Marie looked back to the postcard, remembering all of the postcards she'd discovered in one of June Manor's hidden rooms—postcards that had detailed her mother's travels.

Marie thought she'd hold on to this one and the others that were to come. And maybe she'd send a few back out to June Manor as well. Because if the last year of her life had taught her anything, it was that life was most rewarding when things were unexpected and when she took chances. As far as she was concerned, there would be plenty of postcards to send because even at the age of forty-two, she somehow got the sense that this was only the beginning.

A NEW SERIES!

NOW AVAILABLE!

<u>The Witching Place: A Fatal Folio</u>
(A Curious Bookstore Cozy Mystery—Book 1)

"The perfect romance or beach read, with a difference: its enthusiasm and beautiful descriptions offer an unexpected attention to the complexity of not just evolving love, but evolving psyches. It's a delightful recommendation for romance readers looking for a touch more complexity from their romance reads."
--Midwest Book Review (*For Now and Forever*)

THE WITCHING PLACE: A FATAL FOLIO is the debut novel in a charming new cozy mystery series by bestselling author Sophie Love, author of *The Inn at Sunset Harbor* series, a #1 Bestseller with over 200 five-star reviews.

When Alexis Blair, 29, is fired from her book publishing job and breaks up with her boyfriend on the same day, she wonders if life is urging her to make a fresh start. She decides it's time to pursue her lifelong dream of opening a bookstore of her own—even if that means leaving Boston and accepting a job in a curious bookstore in a small seaside town an hour away.

But the odd shop, Alexis soon learns, is from more than just a rare, occult bookstore. Something strange is going on in the shop's secret back room, with its eccentric owner, and in the small town itself.

And when a dead body appears, Alexis, with her beloved newfound cat, may find herself right in the middle of it all.

A page-turning cozy, rife with the supernatural, mystery, secrets and love—and centered around a small town as odd and endearing as its shop—A CURIOUS BOOKSTORE will make you fall in love and keep you laughing out loud as you turn pages late into the night.

"The romance is there, but not overdosed. Kudos to the author for this amazing start of a series that promises to be very entertaining."
--Books and Movies Reviews (*For Now and Forever*)

Books #2 and #3 in the series—MURDER BY MANUSCRIPT and A PERILOUS PAGE—are now also available!

Sophie Love

#1 bestselling author Sophie Love is author of THE INN AT SUNSET HARBOR romantic comedy series, which includes eight books; of THE ROMANCE CHRONICLES romantic comedy series, which includes five books; of the new CANINE CASPER cozy mystery series, which included six books; and of the new CURIOUS BOOKSTORE cozy mystery series, which included five books (and counting).

Sophie would love to hear from you, so please visit www.sophieloveauthor.com to email her, to join the mailing list, to receive free ebooks, to hear the latest news, and to stay in touch!

BOOKS BY SOPHIE LOVE

A CURIOUS BOOKSTORE COZY MYSTERY
THE WITCHING PLACE: A FATAL FOLIO (Book #1)
THE WITCHING PLACE: MURDER BY MANUSCRIPT (Book #2)
THE WITCHING PLACE: A PERILOUS PAGE (Book #3)
THE WITCHING PLACE: A VANISHED VOLUME (Book #4)
THE WITCHING PLACE: A TAINTED TOME (Book #5)

THE CANINE CASPER COZY MYSTERY SERIES
THE GHOSTLY GROUNDS: MURDER AND BREAKFAST (Book #1)
THE GHOSTLY GROUNDS: DEATH AND BRUNCH (Book #2)
THE GHOSTLY GROUNDS: MALICE AND LUNCH (Book #3)
THE GHOSTLY GROUNDS: VENGEANCE AND DINNER (Book #4)
THE GHOSTLY GROUNDS: SCANDAL AND SUPPER (Book #5)
THE GHOSTLY GROUNDS: DISASTER AND DESSERT (Book #6)

THE INN AT SUNSET HARBOR
FOR NOW AND FOREVER (Book #1)
FOREVER AND FOR ALWAYS (Book #2)
FOREVER, WITH YOU (Book #3)
IF ONLY FOREVER (Book #4)
FOREVER AND A DAY (Book #5)
FOREVER, PLUS ONE (Book #6)
FOR YOU, FOREVER (Book #7)
CHRISTMAS FOREVER (Book #8)

THE ROMANCE CHRONICLES
LOVE LIKE THIS (Book #1)
LOVE LIKE THAT (Book #2)
LOVE LIKE OURS (Book #3)
LOVE LIKE THEIRS (Book #4)
LOVE LIKE YOURS (Book #5)

Made in the USA
Columbia, SC
31 October 2021